THE PLANET SAVERS

Dr. Jay Allison was a surgeon specializing in the parasitology of the planet Darkover. Antiseptic hospital walls were the limits of his world—the virgin ranges of the planet, and its people, were abhorrent to him.

Jason was Dr. Allison's exact opposite—headstrong and impulsive. Raised by the semi-human Trailmen, he loved Darkover as his only known home.

A deadly epidemic threatened the planet, an epidemic that would destroy both Terran and Darkovan civilization, and the only hope for a cure lay somewhere in the unknown vastness of Trailmen territory.

Only Jason could lead them safely through that dangerous land, and only Jay Allison could develop the cure—but it was impossible for them to work together . . . for both minds shared one body.

Plus! THE WATERFALL, a powerful and macabre short story of Darkover making its first appearance in this volume.

THE PLANET SAVERS

by

MARION ZIMMER BRADLEY

ace books

A Division of Charter Communications Inc.
A GROSSET & DUNLAP COMPANY
1120 Avenue of the Americas
New York, New York 10036

Printed in U.S.A.

ACE DARKOVER Novels by Marion Zimmer Bradley:

STAR OF DANGER

THE BLOODY SUN

THE WINDS OF DARKOVER

THE SWORD OF ALDONES

THE PLANET SAVERS

THE WORLD WRECKERS

TO PAUL ZIMMER

TABLE OF CONTENTS

THE PLANET SAVERS   1

THE WATERFALL   103

CHAPTER I

BY THE TIME I got myself all the way awake I thought I was alone. I was lying on a leather couch in a bare white room with huge windows, alternate glass-brick and clear glass. Beyond the clear windows was a view of snow-peaked mountains which turned to pale shadows in the glass-brick.

Habit and memory fitted names to all these. The bare office, the orange flare of the great sun, the names of the dimming mountains. But beyond a polished glass desk, a man sat watching me. And I had never seen the man before.

He was chubby, and not young, and had ginger-colored eyebrows and a fringe of ginger-colored hair around the edges of a forehead which was otherwise quite pink and bald. He was wearing a white uniform coat, and the intertwined caduceus on the pocket and on the sleeve proclaimed him a member of the Medical Service attached to the Civilian HQ of the Terran Trade City.

I didn't stop to make all these evaluations consciously, of course. They were just part of my world when I woke up and found it taking shape around me. The familiar mountains, the familiar sun, the strange man. But he spoke to me in a friendly way, as if it were an ordinary thing to find a perfect stranger sprawled out taking a siesta in here.

"Could I trouble you to tell me your name?"

That was reasonable enough. If I found somebody making himself at home in my office—if I had an office—I'd ask him his name, too. I started to swing my legs to the floor, and had to stop and steady myself with one hand while the room drifted in giddy circles around me.

"I wouldn't try to sit up just yet," he remarked, while the floor calmed down again. Then he repeated, politely but insistently, "Your name?"

"Oh, yes. My name." It was—I fumbled through layers of what felt like gray fuzz, trying to lay my tongue on the most familiar of all sounds, my own name. It was—why, it was—I said, on a high rising note, "This is damn silly," and swallowed. And swallowed again. Hard.

"Calm down," the chubby man said soothingly. That was easier said than done. I stared at him in growing panic and demanded, "But, but, have I had amnesia or something?"

"Or something."

"What's my *name?*"

"Now, now, take it easy! I'm sure you'll remember it soon enough. You can answer other questions, I'm sure. How old are you?"

I answered eagerly and quickly "Twenty-two."

The chubby man scribbled something on a card. "Interesting. In-ter-est-ing. Do you know where we are?"

I looked around the office. "In the Terran Headquarters. From your uniform, I'd say we were on Floor 8—Medical."

He nodded and scribbled again, pursing his lips. "Can you—uh—tell me what planet we are on?"

I had to laugh. "Darkover," I chuckled, "I hope! And if you want the names of the moons, or the date of the founding of the Trade City, or something—"

He gave in, laughing with me. "Remember where you were born?"

2

"On Samarra. I came here when I was three years old—my father was in Mapping and Exploring—" I stopped short, in shock. "He's dead!"

"Can you tell me your father's name?"

"Same as mine. Jay—Jason—" the flash of memory closed down in the middle of a word. It had been a good try, but it hadn't quite worked. The doctor said soothingly, "We're doing very well."

"You haven't told me anything," I accused. "Who are you? Why are you asking me all these questions?"

He pointed to a sign on his desk. I scowled and spelled out the letters. "Randall—Forth—Director—Department—"and Dr. Forth made a note. I said aloud, "It is—*Doctor* Forth, isn't it?"

"Don't you know?"

I looked down at myself, and shook my head. "Maybe *I'm* Doctor Forth," I said, noticing for the first time that I was also wearing a white coat with the caduceus emblem of Medical. But it had the wrong feel, as if I were dressed in somebody else's clothes. *I* was no doctor, was I? I pushed back one sleeve slightly, exposing a long, triangular scar under the cuff. Dr. Forth—by now I was sure *he* was Dr. Forth—followed the direction of my eyes.

"Where did you get the scar?"

"Knife fight. One of the bands of those-who-may-not-enter-cities caught us on the slopes, and we—" the memory thinned out again, and I said despairingly, "It's all confused! What's the matter? Why am I up on Medical? Have I had an accident? Amnesia?"

"Not exactly. I'll explain."

I got up and walked to the window, unsteadily because my feet wanted to walk slowly

3

while I felt like bursting through some invisible net and striding there at one bound. Once I got to the window the room stayed put while I gulped down great breaths of warm sweetish air. I said, "I could use a drink."

"Good idea. Though I don't usually recommend it." Forth reached into a drawer for a flat bottle; poured tea-colored liquid into a throwaway cup. After a minute he poured more for himself. "Here. And sit down, man. You make me nervous, hovering like that."

I didn't sit down. I strode to the door and flung it open. Forth's voice was low and unhurried.

"What's the matter? You can go out, if you want to, but won't you sit down and talk to me for a minute? Anyway, where do you want to go?"

The question made me uncomfortable. I took a couple of long breaths and came back into the room. Forth said, "Drink this," and I poured it down. He refilled the cup unasked, and I swallowed that too and felt the hard lump in my middle began to loosen up and dissolve.

Forth said, "Claustrophobia too. Typical," and scribbled on the card some more. I was getting tired of that performance. I turned on him to tell him so, then suddenly felt amused—or maybe it was the liquor working in me. He seemed such a funny little man, shutting himself up inside an office like this and talking about claustrophobia and watching me as if I were a big bug. I tossed the cup into a disposall.

"Isn't it about time for a few of those explanations?"

"If you think you can take it. How do you feel now?"

4

"Fine." I sat down on the couch again, leaning back and stretching out my long legs comfortably. "What did you put in that drink?"

He chuckled. "Trade secret. Now, the easiest way to explain would be to let you watch a film we made yesterday."

"To watch—" I stopped. "It's your time we're wasting."

He punched a button on the desk, spoke into a mouthpiece. "Surveillance? Give us a monitor on—" he spoke a string of incomprehensible numbers, while I lounged at ease on the couch. Forth waited for an answer, then touched another button and steel louvers closed noiselessly over the windows, blacking them out. The darkness felt oddly more normal than the light, and I leaned back and watched the flickers clear as one wall of the office became a large vision-screen. Forth came and sat beside me on the leather couch, but in the picture Forth was there, sitting at his desk, watching another man, a stranger, walk into the office.

Like Forth, the newcomer wore a white coat with the caduceus emblems. I disliked the man on sight. He was tall and lean and composed, with a dour face set in thin lines. I guessed that he was somewhere in his thirties. Dr. Forth-in-the-film said, "Sit down, doctor," and I drew a long breath, overwhelmed by a curious sensation.

I have been here before. I have seen this happen before.

(And curiously formless I felt. I sat and watched, and I knew I was watching, and sitting. But it was in that dreamlike fashion, where the dreamer at once watches his visions and participates in them . . .)

"Sit down, doctor," Forth said. "Did you bring in the reports?"

Jay Allison carefully took the indicated seat, poised nervously on the edge of the chair. He sat very straight, leaning forward only a little to hand a thick folder of papers across the desk. Forth took it, but didn't open it. "What do you think, Dr. Allison?"

"There is no possible room for doubt." Jay Allison spoke precisely, in a rather high-pitched and emphatic tone. "It follows the statistical pattern for all recorded attacks of 48-year fever—by the way, sir, haven't we any better name than that for this particular disease? The term '48-year fever' connotes a fever of 48 years' duration, rather than a pandemic recurring every 48 years."

"A fever that lasted 48 years would be quite a fever," Dr. Forth said with a grim smile. "Nevertheless that's the only name we have so far. Name it and you can have it. Allison's disease?"

Jay Allison greeted this pleasantry with a repressive frown. "As I understand it, the disease cycle seems to be connected somehow with the once-every-48-years' conjunction of the four moons, which explains why the Darkovans are so superstitious about it. The moons have remarkably eccentric orbits—I don't know anything about that part, I'm quoting Dr. Moore. If there's an animal vector to the disease, we've never discovered it. The pattern runs like this; a few cases in the mountain districts, the next month a hundred-odd cases all over this part of the planet. Then it skips exactly three months without increase. The next upswing puts the number of the reported cases in the thousands, and three months after *that*, it reaches real pandemic proportions and decimates the entire human population of Darkover."

"That's about it," Forth admitted. They bent together over the folder, Jay Allison drawing back slightly to avoid touching the other man.

Forth said, "We Terrans have a Trade compact on Darkover for a hundred and fifty-two years. The first outbreak of this 48-year fever killed all but a dozen men out of three hundred. The Darkovans were worse off than we were. The last outbreak wasn't as bad, but it was bad enough, I've heard. It had an eighty-seven percent mortality—for humans, that is. I understand the Trailmen don't die of it."

"The Darkovans call it the Trailmen's fever, Dr. Forth, because the Trailmen are virtually immune to it. It remains in their midst as a mild ailment taken by children. When it breaks out into a virulent form every 48 years, most of the Trailmen are already immune. I took the disease myself as a child —maybe you heard?"

Forth nodded. "You may be the only Terran ever to contract the disease and survive."

"The Trailmen incubate the disease," Jay Allison said. "I should think the logical thing would be to drop a couple of hydrogen bombs on the trail cities —and wipe it out for good and all."

(Sitting on the sofa in Forth's dark office, I stiffened with such fury that he shook my shoulder and muttered "Easy, there, man!")

Dr. Forth, on the screen, looked annoyed, and Jay Allison said, with a grimace of distaste, "I didn't mean that literally. But the Trailmen are not human. It wouldn't be genocide, just an exterminator's job. A public health measure."

Forth looked shocked as he realized that the

7

younger man meant what he was saying. He said, "Galactic Center would have to rule on whether they're dumb animals or intelligent nonhumans, and whether they're entitled to the status of a civilization. All precedent on Darkover is toward recognizing them as men—and good God, Jay, you'd probably be called as a witness for the defense! How can you say they're not human after your experience with them? Anyway, by the time their status was finally decided, half of the recognizable humans on Darkover would be dead. We need a better solution than that."

He pushed his chair back and looked out the window.

"I won't go into this political situation," he said, "You aren't interested in Terran Empire politics, and I'm no expert either. But you'd have to be deaf, dumb and blind not to know that Darkover's been playing the immovable object to the irresistible force. The Darkovans are more advanced in some of the non-causative sciences than we are and, until now, they wouldn't admit that Terra had a thing to contribute. However—and this is the big however—they do know, and they're willing to admit, that our medical sciences are better than theirs."

"Theirs being practically nonexistent."

"Exactly—and this could be the first crack in the barrier. You may not realize the significance of this, but the Legate received an offer from the Hasturs themselves."

Jay Allison murmured, "I'm to be impressed?"

"On Darkover you'd damn well better be impressed when the Hasturs sit up and take notice."

"I understand they're telepaths or something—"

"Telepaths, psychokinetics, parapsychs, just about

anything else. For all practical purposes they're the Gods of Darkover. And one of the Hasturs—a rather young and unimportant one, I'll admit, the old man's grandson—came to the Legate's office, in person, mind you. He offered, if the Terran Medical would help Darkover lick the Trailmen's fever, to coach selected Terran men in matrix mechanics."

"Good God," Jay said. It was a concession beyond Terra's wildest dreams; for a hundred years they had tried to beg, buy or steal some knowledge of the mysterious science of matrix mechanics—that curious discipline which could turn matter into raw energy, and vice versa, without any intermediate stages and without fission by-products. Matrix mechanics had made the Darkovans virtually immune to the lure of Terra's advanced technologies.

Jay said, "Personally I think Darkovan science is overrated. But I can see the propaganda angle—"

"Not to mention the humanitarian angle of healing."

Jay Allison gave one of his cold shrugs. "The real angle seems to be this: *can* we cure the 48-year fever?"

"Not yet. But we have a lead. During the last epidemic, a Terran scientist discovered a blood fraction containing antibodies against the fever—in the Trailmen. Isolated to a serum, it might reduce the virulent 48-year epidemic form to the mild form again. Unfortunately, he died himself in the epidemic, without finishing his work, and his notebooks were overlooked until this year. We have 18,000 men, and their families, on Darkover now, Jay. Frankly, if we lose too many of them, we're going to have to pull out of Darkover—the big brass on Terra will write off the loss of a garrison of professional traders, but not of a whole Trade City colony. That's not even mentioning the prestige we'll lose if our much-vaunted Terran medical sciences can't save Darkover from an epidemic. We've got exactly five months. We can't synthesize a serum in that time. We've got to appeal to the Trailmen. And that's why I called you up here. You know more about the Trailmen than any living Terran. You ought to. You spent eight years in a Nest."

(In Forth's darkened office I sat up straighter, with a flash of returning memory. Jay Allison, I judged, was several years older than I, but we had one thing in common; this cold fish of a man shared with myself that experience of marvelous years spent in an alien world!)

Jay Allison scowled, displeased. "That was years ago. I was hardly more than a baby. My father crashed on a Mapping expedition over the Hellers —God only knows what possessed him to try and take a light plane over those crosswinds. I survived the crash by the merest chance, and lived with the Trailmen—so I'm told—until I was thirteen or fourteen. I don't remember much about it. Children aren't particularly observant."

Forth leaned over the desk, staring. "You speak their language, don't you?"

"I used to. I might remember it under hypnosis, I suppose. Why? Do you want me to translate something?"

"Not exactly. We were thinking of sending you on an expedition to the Trailmen themselves."

(In the darkened office, watching Jay's startled face, I thought, God, what an adventure! I wonder —I wonder if they want me to go with him?)

Forth was explaining; "It would be a difficult trek. You know what the Hellers are like. Still, you used to climb mountains, as a hobby, before you went into Medical—"

"I outgrew the childishness of hobbies many years ago, sir," Jay said stiffly.

"We'd get you the best guides we could, Terran and Darkovan. But they couldn't do the one thing you can do. You *know* the Trailmen, Jay. You might be able to persuade them to do the one thing they've never done before."

"What's that?" Jay Allison sounded suspicious.

"Come out of the mountains. Send us volunteers —blood donors—we might, if we had enough blood to work on, be able to isolate the right fraction, and synthesize it, in time to prevent the epidemic from really taking hold, Jay. It's a tough mission and it's dangerous as all hell, but somebody's got to do it, and I'm afraid you're the only qualified man."

"I like my first suggestion better. Bomb the Trailmen—and the Hellers—right off the planet." Jay's face was set in lines of loathing, which he controlled after a minute, and said, "I—I didn't mean that. Theoretically I can see the necessity, only—" he stopped and swallowed.

"Please say what you were going to say."

"I wonder if I am as well qualified as you think? No—don't interrupt—I find the natives of Darkover distasteful, even the humans. As for the Trailmen—"

(I was getting mad and impatient. I whispered to Forth in the darkness "Shut the goddam film off! You couldn't send *that* guy on an errand like *that*! I'd rather—"

Forth snapped "Shut up and listen!"

I shut up.)

Jay Allison was not acting. He was pained and disgusted. Forth wouldn't let him finish his explanation of why he had refused even to teach in the Medical College established for Darkovans by the Terran empire. He interrupted, and he sounded irritated,

"We know all that. It evidently never occurred to you, Jay, that it's an inconvenience to us—that all this vital knowledge should lie, purely by accident, in the hands of the one man who's too damned stubborn to use it?"

Jay didn't move an eyelash, where I would have squirmed "I have always been aware of that, doctor."

Forth drew a long breath. "I'll concede you're not suitable at the moment, Jay. But what do you know of applied psychodynamics?"

"Very little I'm sorry to say." Allison didn't sound sorry, though. He sounded bored to death with the whole conversation.

"May I be blunt—and personal?"

"Please do. I'm not at all sensitive."

"Basically, then, Doctor Allison, a person as contained and repressed as yourself usually has a clearly defined subsidiary personality. In neurotic individuals this complex of personality traits sometimes splits off, and we get a syndrome known as multiple, or alternate personality."

"I've scanned a few of the classic cases. Wasn't there a woman with four separate personalities?"

"Exactly. However, you aren't neurotic, and ordinarily there would not be the slightest chance of your repressed alternate taking over your personality."

12

"Thank you," Jay murmured ironically, "I'd be losing sleep over that."

"Nevertheless I presume you *do* have such a subsidiary personality, although he would normally manifest. This subsidiary—let's call him Jay—would embody all the characteristics which you repress. He would be gregarious, where you are retiring and studious; adventurous where you are cautious; talkative while you are taciturn; he would perhaps enjoy action for its own sake, while you exercise faithfully in the gymnasium only for your health's sake; and he might even remember the Trailmen with pleasure rather than dislike."

"In short—a blend of all the undesirable characteristics?"

"One could put it that way. Certainly, he would be a blend of all the characteristics which you, Jay, *consider* undesirable. But—if released by hypnotism and suggestion, he might be suitable for the job in hand."

"But how do you know I actually have such an —alternate?"

"I don't. But it's a good guess. Most repressed—" Forth coughed and amended "most *disciplined* personalities possess such a suppressed secondary personality. Don't you occasionally—rather rarely—find yourself doing things which are entirely out of character for you?"

I could almost feel Allison taking it in, as he confessed, "Well—yes. For instance, the other day, although I dress conservatively at all times—" he glanced at his uniform coat, "I found myself buying—" he stopped again and his face went an unlovely terra-cotta color as he finally mumbled "a lowered red sport shirt."

Sitting in the dark I felt vaguely sorry for the poor gawk, disturbed by, ashamed of the only human impulses he ever had. On the screen Allison frowned fiercely. "A—crazy impulse."

"You could say that, or say it was an action of the suppressed Jay. How about it, Allison? You may be the only Terran on Darkover, maybe the only human, who could get into a Trailman's Nest without being murdered."

"Sir—as a citizen of the Empire, I don't have any choice, do I?"

"Jay, look," Forth said, and I felt him trying to reach through the barricade and touch, really touch that cold, contained young man, "We couldn't *order* any man to do anything like this. Aside from the ordinary dangers, it could destroy your personal balance, maybe permanently. I'm asking you to volunteer something above and beyond the call of duty. Man to man—what do you say?"

I would have been moved by his words. Even at second hand I was moved by them. Jay Allison looked at the floor and I saw him twist his long well-kept surgeon's hands and crack the knuckles with an odd gesture. Finally he said, "I haven't any choice either way, doctor. I'll take the chance. I'll go to the Trailmen."

CHAPTER II

THE SCREEN went dark again and Forth flicked the light on. He said "Well?"

I gave it back, in his own intonation, "Well?" and was exasperated to find that I was twisting my own knuckles in the nervous gesture of Allison's painful decision. I jerked them apart and got up.

"I suppose it didn't work, with that cold fish, and you decided to come to me instead? Sure, *I'll* go to the Trailmen for you. Not with that Allison bastard —I wouldn't go anywhere with that guy—but I speak the Trailmen's language, and without hypnosis, either."

Forth was staring at me. "So you've remembered that?"

"Hell yes," I said, "My Dad crashed in the Hellers, and a band of Trailmen found me, half dead. I lived there until I was about fifteen, then their Old-One decided I was too human for 'em, and they took me out through Dammerung Pass and arranged to have me brought here. Sure, it's all coming back now. I spent five years in the Spacemen's Orphanage, then I went to work taking Terran tourists on hunting parties and so on, because I liked being around the mountains. I—" I stopped. Forth was staring at me.

"Sit down again, won't you? Can't you keep still a minute?" Reluctantly, I sat down. "You think you'd like this job?"

"It would be tough," I said, considering. "The People of the Sky—" (using the Trailmen's name for themselves) "—don't like outsiders, but they might be persuaded. The worst part would be getting there. The plane, or the 'copter, isn't built that can get through the crosswinds around the Hellers, and land inside them. We'd have to go on foot, all the way from Carthon. I'd need professional climbers— mountaineers."

"Then you don't share Allison's attitude?"

"Dammit, don't insult me!" I discovered that I

was on my feet again, pacing the office restlessly. Forth stared and mused aloud, "What's personality anyway? A mask of emotions, superimposed on the body and the intellect. Change the point of view, change the emotions and desires, and even with the same body and the same past experiences, you have a new man."

I swung around in mid-step. A new and terrible suspicion, too monstrous to name, was creeping up on me. Forth touched a button and the face of Jay Allison, immobile, appeared on the vision-screen. Forth put a mirror in my hand. He said "Jason Allison, look at yourself."

I looked.

"No," I said. And again, "No. No. No."

Forth didn't argue. He pointed, with a stubby finger. "Look—" he moved the finger as he spoke, "Height of forehead. Set of cheekbones. Your eyebrows look different, and your mouth, because the expression is different. But bone structure—the nose, the chin—"

I heard myself make a queer sound; dashed the mirror to the floor. He grabbed my forearm. "Steady, man!"

I found a scrap of my voice. It didn't sound like Allison's. "Then I'm—Jay? Jay Allison with amnesia?"

"Not exactly." Forth mopped his forehead with an immaculate sleeve and it came away damp with sweat, "God, no, *not* Jay Allison as I know him!" He drew a long breath. "And sit down. Whoever you are, sit *down!*"

I sat. Gingerly. Not sure.

"But the man Jay might have been, given a different temperamental bias. I'd say—the man Jay Allison started out to be. The man he *refused* to be. Within his subconscious, he built up barriers against a whole series of memories, and the subliminal threshhold—"

"Doc, I don't understand the psycho talk."

Forth stared. "And you do remember the Trailmen's language. I thought so. Allison's personality is suppressed in you, as yours was in him."

"One thing, Doc. I don't know a thing about blood fractions or epidemics. My half of the personality didn't study medicine." I took up the mirror again and broodingly studied the face there. The high thin cheeks, high forehead shaded by coarse, dark hair which Jay Allison had slicked down, now heavily rumpled. I still didn't think I looked anything like the doctor. Our voices were nothing alike either. His had been pitched rather high. My own, as nearly as I could judge, was a full octave deeper, and more resonant. Yet they issued from the same vocal chords, unless Forth were having a reasonless, macabre joke.

"Did I honest-to-God study medicine? It's the last thing I'd think about. It's an honest trade, I guess, but I've never been that intellectual."

"You—or rather, Jay Allison is a specialist in Darkovan parasitology, as well as a very competent surgeon." Forth was sitting with his chin in his hands, watching me intently. He scowled and said, "If anything, the physical change is more startling than the other. I wouldn't have recognized you."

"That tallies with me. I don't recognize myself," I added, "—and the queer thing is, I didn't even *like* Jay Allison, to put it mildly. If he—I can't say *he*, can I?"

"I don't know why not. You're no more Jay Allison

17

than I am. For one thing, you're younger. Ten years younger. I doubt if any of his friends—if he had any —would recognize you. You—it's ridiculous to go on calling you Jay. What should I call you?"

"Why should I care? Call me Jason."

"Suits you," Forth said enigmatically. "Look, then, Jason. I'd like to give you a few days to readjust to your new personality, but we are really pressed for time. Can you fly to Carthon tonight? I've hand-picked a good crew for you, and sent them on ahead. You'll meet them there."

I stared at him. Suddenly the room oppressed me and I found it hard to breathe. I said in wonder "You were pretty sure of yourself, weren't you?"

Forth just looked at me, for what seemed a long time. Then he said, in a very quiet voice "No. I wasn't sure at all. But if you didn't turn up, and I couldn't talk Jay into it, I'd have had to try it myself."

Jason Allison, Junior, was listed on the directory of the Terran HQ as "Suite 1214, Medical Residence Corridor." I found the rooms without any trouble, though an elderly doctor stared at me rather curiously as I barged along the quiet hallway. The suite —bedroom, miniscule sitting-room, compact bath— depressed me: clean, closed-in and neutral as the man who owned them. I rummaged through them restlessly, trying to find some scrap of familiarity to indicate that I had lived here for the past eleven years.

Jay Allison was thirty-four years old. I had given my age, without hesitation, as twenty-two. There were no obvious blanks in my memory; from the moment Jay Allison had spoken of the Trailmen, my past had rushed back and stood, complete to yesterday's supper (only had I eaten that supper twelve years ago?). I remembered my father, a lined, silent man who had liked to fly often, taking photograph after photograph from his plane for the meticulous work of Mapping and Exploration. He'd liked to have me fly with him and I'd flown over virtually every inch of the planet. No one else had ever dared fly over the Hellers, except the big commercial spacecraft that kept to a safe altitude. I vaguely remembered the crash and the strange hands pulling me out of the wreckage and the weeks I'd spent, broken-bodied and delirious, gently tended by one of the red-eyed, twittering women of the Trailmen. In all, I had spent eight years in the Nest, which was not a nest at all, but a vast sprawling city built in the branches of enormous trees. With the small and delicate humanoids who had been my playfellows, I had gathered the nuts and buds and trapped the small arboreal animals they used for food, taken my share at weaving clothing from the fibres of parasite plants cultivated on the stems, and in all those eight years I had set foot on the ground less than a dozen times, even though I had travelled for miles through the tree-roads high above the forest floor.

Then the Old-One's painful decision that I was too alien for them, and the difficult and dangerous journey my Trailmen foster-parents and foster-brothers had undertaken, to help me out of the Hellers and arrange for me to be taken to the Trade City. After two years of physically painful and mentally rebellious readjustment to daytime living (the owl-eyed Trailmen saw best, and lived largely, by moonlight) I had found a niche for myself, and settled down. But all of the later years (after Jay Allison had taken over, I supposed, from a basic pattern of memory common to both of us) had vanished into the limbo of the subconscious.

A bookrack was crammed with large microcards; I slipped one into the viewer, with a queer sense of spying, and found myself listening apprehensively to hear that measured step and Jay Allison's shrill voice demanding what the hell I was doing, meddling with his possessions. Eye to the viewer, I read briefly at random, something about the management of compound fracture, then realized I had understood exactly three words in a paragraph. I put my fist against my forehead and heard the words echoing there emptily; "laceration . . . primary efflusion . . . serum and lympth . . . granulation tissue . . ." I presumed that the words meant something and that I once had known what. But if I had a medical education, I didn't recall a syllable of it. I didn't know a fracture from a fraction.

In a sudden frenzy of impatience I stripped off the white coat and put on the first shirt I came to, a crimson thing that hung in the line of white coats like an exotic bird in snow country. I went back to rummaging the drawers and bureaus. Carelessly shoved in a pigeonhole I found another microcard that looked familiar, and when I slipped it mechanically into the viewer it turned out to be a book on mountaineering which, oddly enough, I remembered buying as a youngster. It dispelled my last, lingering doubts. Evidently I had bought it before the personalities had forked so sharply apart and separated, Jason from Jay. I was beginning to believe. Not to accept. Just to believe it had happened. The book looked well-thumbed, and had been handled so much I had to baby it into the slot of the viewer.

Under a folded pile of clean underwear I found a flat half-empty bottle of whisky. I remembered Forth's words that he'd never seen Jay Allison drink, and suddenly I thought "The poor fool!" I fixed myself a drink and sat down, idly scanning the mountaineering book.

Not till I'd entered medical school, I suspected, did the two halves of me fork so strongly apart—so strongly that there had been days and weeks and, I suspected, years when Jay Allison had kept me prisoner. I tried to juggle dates in my mind, looked at a calendar, and got such a mental jolt that I put it face-down to think about when I was a little drunker.

I wondered if my detailed memories of my teens and early twenties were the same memories Jay Allison looked back on. I didn't think so. People forget and remember selectively. Week by week, then, and year by year, the dominant personality of Jay had crowded me out; so that the young rowdy, more than half Darkovan, loving the mountains, half homesick for a non-human world, had been drowned in the chilly, austere young medical student who lost himself in his work. But I, Jason—I had always been the watcher behind, the person Jay Allison dared not be? Why was he past thirty —and I just 22?

A ringing shattered the silence; I had to hunt for the intercom on the bedroom wall. I said, "Who is it?" and an unfamiliar voice demanded "Dr. Allison?"

I said automatically "Nobody here by that name,"

and started to put back the mouthpiece. Then I stopped and gulped and asked, "Is that you, Dr. Forth?"

It was, and I breathed again. I didn't even want to think about what I'd say if somebody else demanded to know why the devil I was answering Dr. Allison's private telephone. When Forth had finished, I went to the mirror, and stared, trying to see behind my face the sharp features of that stranger, *Doctor* Jason Allison. I delayed, even while I was wondering what few things I should pack for a trip into the mountains, and the habit of hunting parties was making mental lists about heat-socks and windbreakers. The face that looked at me was a young face, unlined and faintly freckled, the same face as always except that I'd lost my suntan; Jay Allison had kept me indoors too long. Suddenly I struck the mirror lightly with my fist.

"The hell with you, Dr. Allison," I said, and went to see if he had kept any clothes fit to pack.

CHAPTER III

DR. FORTH was waiting for me in the small skyport on the roof, and so was a small 'copter, one of the fairly old ones assigned to Medical Service when they were too beat up for services with higher priority. Forth took one startled look at my crimson shirt, but all he said was "Hello, Jason. Here's something we've got to decide right away; do we tell the crew who you really are?"

I shook my head emphatically. "I'm not Jay Allison; I don't want his name or his reputation. Unless there are men on the crew who know Allison by sight—"

"Some of them do, but I don't think they'd recognize you."

"Tell them I'm his twin brother," I said humorlessly.

"That wouldn't be necessary. There's not enough resemblance." Forth raised his head and beckoned to a man who was doing something near the 'copter. He said under his breath "You'll see what I mean," as the man approached.

He wore the uniform of Spaceforce—black leather with a little rainbow of stars on his sleeve meaning he'd seen service on a dozen different planets, a different colored star for each one. He wasn't a young man, but on the wrong side of fifty, seamed and burly and huge, with a split lip and weathered face. I liked his looks. We shook hands and Forth said, "This is our man, Kendricks. He's called Jason, and he's an expert on the Trailmen. Jason, this is Buck Kendricks."

"Glad to know you, Jason." I thought Kendricks looked at me half a second more than necessary. "The 'copter's ready. Climb in, Doc—you're going as far as Carthon, aren't you?"

We put on zippered windbreakers and the 'copter soared noiselessly into the pale crimson sky. I sat beside Forth, looking down through pale lilac clouds at the pattern of Darkover spread below me.

"Kendricks was giving me a funny eye, Doc. What's biting him?"

"He has known Jay Allison for eight years," Forth said quietly, "and he hasn't recognized you yet."

But we let it ride at that, to my great relief, and

didn't talk any more about me at all. As we flew under silent whirring blades, turning our backs on the settled country which lay near the Trade City, we talked about Darkover itself. Forth told me about the Trailmen's fever and managed to give me some idea about what the blood fraction was, and why it was necessary to persuade fifty or sixty of the humanoids to return with me, to donate blood from which the antibody could be first isolated, then synthesized.

It would be a totally unheard-of thing, if I could accomplish it. Most of the Trailmen never touched ground in their entire lives, except when crossing the passes above the snow line. Not a dozen of them, including my foster parents, who had so painfully brought me out across Dammerung, had ever crossed the ring of encircling mountains that walled them away from the rest of the planet. Humans sometimes penetrated the lower forests in search of the Trailmen. It was one-way traffic. The Trailmen never came in search of *them*.

We talked, too, about some of those humans who had crossed the mountains into Trailmen country—those mountains profanely dubbed the Hellers by the first Terrans who had tried to fly over them in anything lower or slower than a spaceship.

"What about this crew you picked? They're not Terrans?"

Forth shook his head. "It would be murder to send anyone recognizably Terran into the Hellers. You know how the Trailmen feel about outsiders getting into their country." I knew. Forth continued, "Just the same, there will be two Terrans with you."

"They don't know Jay Allison?" I didn't want to

24

be burdened with anyone—not anyone—who would
know me, or expect me to behave like my forgotten
other self.

"Kendricks knows you," Forth said, "but I'm going to be perfectly truthful. I never knew Jay Allison well, except in line of work. I know a lot of
things—from the past couple of days—which came
out during the hypnotic sessions, which he'd never
have dreamed of telling me, or anyone else, consciously. And that comes under the heading of a
professional confidence—even from you. And for
that reason, I'm sending Kendricks along—and
you're going to have to take the chance he'll recognize you. Isn't that Carthon down there?"

Carthon lay nestled under the outlying foothills
of the Hellers, ancient and sprawling and squatty,
and burned brown with the dust of five thousand
years. Children ran out to stare at the 'copter as we
landed near the city; few planes ever flew low
enough to be seen, this near the Hellers.

Forth had sent his crew ahead and parked them
in an abandoned huge place at the edge of the city
which might once have been a warehouse or a
ruined palace. Inside there were a couple of trucks,
stripped down to framework and flatbed, like all
machinery shipped through space from Terra. There
were pack animals, dark shapes in the gloom. Crates
were stacked up in an orderly untidiness, and at
the far end a fire was burning and five or six men
in Darkovan clothing—loose-sleeved shirts, tight-
wrapped breeches, low boots—were squatting
around it, talking. They got up as Forth and Kendricks and I walked toward them, and Forth greeted
them clumsily in badly accented Darkovan, then

switched to Terran Standard, letting one of the men translate for him.

Forth introduced me simply as "Jason", after the Darkovan custom, and I looked the men over, one by one. Back when I'd climbed for fun, I'd liked to pick my own men; but whoever had picked this crew must have known his business.

Three were mountain Darkovans, lean swart men enough alike to be brothers; I learned after a while that they actually were brothers, Hjalmar, Garin and Vardo. All three were well over six feet, and Hjalmar stood head and shoulders over his brothers, whom I never learned to tell apart. The fourth man, a redhead, was dressed rather better than the others and introduced as Lerrys Ridenow—the double name indicating high Darkovan aristocracy. He looked muscular and agile enough, but his hands were suspiciously well-kept for a mountain man, and I wondered how much experience he'd had.

The fifth man shook hands with me, speaking to Kendricks and Forth as if they were old friends. "Don't I know you from someplace, Jason?"

He looked Darkovan, and wore Darkovan clothes, but Forth had forewarned me, and attack seemed the best defense. "Aren't you Terran?"

"My father was," he said, and I understood; a situation not exactly uncommon, but ticklish on a planet like Darkover. I said carelessly, "I may have seen you around the HQ. I can't place you, though."

"My name's Rafe Scott. I thought I knew most of the professional guides on Darkover, but I admit I don't get into the Hellers much," he confessed. "Which route are we going to take?"

I found myself drawn into the middle of the group of men, accepting one of the small, sweetish

Darkovan cigarettes, looking over the plan somebody had scribbled down on the top of a packing
case. I borrowed a pencil from Rafe and bent over
the case, sketching out a rough map of the terrain
I remembered so well from boyhood. I might be
bewildered about blood fractions, but when it came
to climbing I knew what I was doing. Rafe and Lerrys and the Darkovan brothers crowded behind me
to look over the sketch, and Lerrys put a long finger-
nail on the route I'd indicated.

"Your elevation's pretty bad here," he said diffi-
dently, "and on the 'Narr campaign the Trailmen
attacked us here, and it was bad fighting along
those ledges."

I looked at him with new respect; dainty hands
or not, he evidently knew the country. Kendricks
patted the blaster on his hip and said grimly, "But
this isn't the 'Narr campaign. I'd like to see any
Trailmen attack us while I have this."

"But you're not going to have it," said a voice behind us, a crisp authoritative voice. "Take off that
gun, man!"

Kendricks and I whirled together to see the
speaker, a tall young Darkovan, still standing in the
shadows. The newcomer spoke to me directly:

"I'm told you are Terran, but that you understand the Trailmen. Surely you don't intend to carry
fission or fusion weapons against them?"

And I suddenly realized that we were in Darkovan territory now, and that we must reckon with
the Darkovan horror of guns or of any weapon
which reaches beyond the arm's length of the man
who wields it. A simple heat-gun, to the Darkovan
ethical code, is as reprehensible as a super-cobalt
planetbuster.

Kendricks protested, "We can't travel unarmed through Trailmen country! We're apt to meet hostile bands of the creatures—and they're nasty with those long knives they carry!"

The stranger said calmly "I've no objection to you, or anyone else, carrying a knife for self-defense."

"A *knife?*" Kendricks drew breath to roar. "Listen, you bug-eyed son of a—who do you think you are, anyway?"

The Darkovans muttered. The man in the shadows said, "Regis Hastur."

Kendricks stared pop-eyed. My own eyes could have popped, but I decided it was time for me to take charge, if I were ever going to. I rapped, "All right, this is my show. Buck, give me the gun."

He looked wrathfully at me for the space of seconds, while I wondered what I'd do if he didn't. Then, slowly, he unbuckled the straps and handed it to me, butt first.

I'd never realized how undressed a Spaceforce man looked without his blaster. I balanced it on my palm for a minute while Regis Hastur came out of the shadows. He was tall, and had the reddish hair and fair skin of Darkovan aristocracy, and on his face was some indefinable stamp—arrogance, perhaps, or the consciousness that the Hasturs had ruled this world for centuries long before the Terrans brought ships and trade and the universe to their doors. He was looking at me as if he approved of me, and that was one step worse than the former situation.

So, using the respectful Darkovan idiom of speaking to a superior (which he was) but keeping my voice hard, I said "There's just one leader on my trek, Lord Hastur. On this one, I'm it. If you want to discuss whether or not we carry guns, I suggest you discuss it with me in private—and let me give the orders."

One of the Darkovans gasped. I knew I could have been mobbed. But with a mixed bag of men, I had to grab leadership quickly or be relegated to nowhere. I didn't give Regis Hastur a chance to answer that, either; I said, "Come back here. I want to talk to you anyway."

He came, and I remembered to breathe. I led the way to a fairly deserted corner of the immense place, faced him and demanded, "As for you—what are you doing here? You're not intending to cross the mountains with us?"

He met my scowl levelly. "I certainly am."

I groaned. "Why? You're the Regent's grandson. Important people don't take on this kind of dangerous work. If anything happens to you, it will be my responsibility!" I was going to have enough trouble, I was thinking, without shepherding along one of the most revered personages on the whole damned planet! I didn't want anyone around who had to be fawned on, or deferred to, or even listened to.

He frowned slightly, and I had the unpleasant impression that he knew what I was thinking. "In the first place, it will mean something to the Trailmen, won't it, to have a Hastur with you, suing for this favor?"

It certainly would. The Trailmen paid little enough heed to the ordinary humans, except for considering them fair game for plundering when they came uninvited into Trailmen country. But they, with all Darkover, revered the Hasturs, and

29

it was a fine point of diplomacy. If the Darkovans sent their most important leader, they might listen to him.

"In the second place," Regis Hastur continued, "the Darkovans are my people, and it's my business to negotiate for them. In the third place, I know the Trailmen's dialect—not well, but I can speak it a little. And in the fourth, I've climbed mountains all my life. Purely as an amateur, but I can assure you I won't be in the way."

There was little enough I could say to that. He seemed to have covered every point—or every point but one, and he added, shrewdly, after a minute, "Don't worry; I'm perfectly willing to have you take charge. I won't claim—privilege."

I had to be satisfied with that.

Darkover is a civilized planet with a fairly high standard of living, but it is not a mechanized or a technological culture. The people don't do much mining, or build factories, and the few which were founded by Terran enterprise never were very successful; outside the Terran Trade City, machinery or modern transportation is almost unknown.

While the other men checked and loaded supplies and Rafe Scott went out to contact some friends of his and arrange for last-minute details, I sat down with Forth to memorize the medical details I must put so clearly to the Trailmen.

"If we could only have kept your medical knowledge!"

"Trouble is, being a doctor doesn't suit my personality," I said. I felt absurdly light-hearted. Where I sat, I could raise my head and study the panorama of blackish-green foothills which lay beyond

Carthon, and search out the stone roadway, like a tiny white ribbon, which we could follow for the first stage of the trip. Forth evidently did not share my enthusiasm.

"You know, Jason, there is one real danger—"

"Do you think I care about danger? Or are you afraid I'll turn—foolhardy?"

"Not exactly. It's not a physical danger, Jason. It's an emotional—or rather an intellectual danger."

"Hell, don't you know any language but that psycho doubletalk?"

"Let me finish, Jason. Jay Allison may have been repressed, overcontrolled, but you are seriously impulsive. You lack a balance-wheel, if I could put it that way. And if you run too many risks, your buried alter-ego may come to the surface and take over in sheer self-preservation."

"In other words," I said, laughing loudly, "if I scare that Allison stuffed-shirt, he may start stirring in his grave?"

Forth coughed and smothered a laugh and said that was one way of putting it. I clapped him reassuringly on the shoulder and said "Forget it, sir. I promise to be godly, sober and industrious—but is there any law against enjoying what I'm doing?"

Somebody burst out of the warehouse-palace place, and shouted at me. "Jason? The guide is here," and I stood up, giving Forth a final grin. "Don't you worry. Jay Allison's good riddance," I said, and went back to meet the other guide they had chosen.

And I almost backed out when I saw the guide. For the guide was a woman.

She was small for a Darkovan girl, and narrowly built, the sort of body that could have been called boyish or coltish but certainly not, at first glance, feminine. Close-cut curls, blue-black and wispy, cast the faintest of shadows over a squarish sunburnt face, and her eyes were so thickly rimmed with heavy dark lashes that I could not guess their color. Her nose was snubbed and might have looked whimsical and was instead oddly arrogant. Her mouth was wide, and her chin round.

She held up her palm and said rather sullenly, "Kyla Rainéach, free Amazon, licensed guide."

I acknowledged the gesture with a nod, scowling. The guild of free Amazons entered virtually every field, but that of mountain guide seemed somewhat bizarre even for an Amazon. She seemed wiry and agile enough, her body, under the heavy blanket-like clothing, almost as lean of hip and flat of breast as my own; only the slender long legs were unequivocally feminine.

The other men were checking and loading supplies; I noted from the corner of my eye that Regis Hastur was taking his turn heaving bundles with the rest. I sat down on some still-undisturbed sacks, and motioned her to sit.

"You've had trail experience? We're going into the Hellers through Dammerung, and that's rough going even for professionals."

She said in a flat expressionless voice, "I was with the Terran Mapping expedition to the South Polar ridge last year."

"Ever been in the Hellers? If anything happened to me, could you lead the expedition safely back to Carthon?"

She looked down at her stubby fingers. "I'm sure I could," she said finally, and started to rise. "Is that all?"

"One more thing—" I gestured to her to stay put. "Kyla, you'll be one woman among eight men—"

The snubbed nose wrinkled up. "I don't expect you to crawl into my blankets, if that's what you mean. It's not in my contract—I hope!"

I felt my face burning. Damn the girl! "It's not in mine, anyway," I snapped, "but I can't answer for seven other men, most of them mountain roughnecks." Even as I said it I wondered why I bothered; certainly a free Amazon could defend her own virtue, or not, if she wanted to, without any help from me. I had to excuse myself by adding, "In either case you'll be a disturbing element—I don't want fights either!"

She made a little low-pitched sound of amusement. "There's safety in numbers, and—are you familiar with the physiological effect of high altitudes on men acclimated to low ones?" Suddenly she threw back her head and the hidden sound became free and merry laughter. "Jason, I'm a free Amazon, and that means—no, I'm not neutered, though some of us are. But you have my word, I won't create any trouble of any recognizably female variety." She stood up. "Now, if you don't mind, I'd like to check the mountain equipment."

Her eyes were still laughing at me, but curiously I didn't mind at all.

CHAPTER IV

WE STARTED that night, a curiously lopsided little caravan. The pack animals were loaded into one truck and didn't like it. We had another stripped-down truck which carried supplies. The ancient stone roads, rutted and gullied here and there with the flood-waters and silt of decades, had not been planned for any travel other than the feet of men or beasts. We passed tiny villages and isolated country estates, and a few of the solitary towers where the matrix mechanics worked alone with the secret sciences of Darkover, towers of unpolished stone which sometimes shone like blue beacons in the dark.

Kendricks drove the truck which carried the animals, and was amused by it. Rafe and I took turns driving the other truck, sharing the wide front seat with Regis Hastur and Kyla, while the other men found seats between crates and sacks in the back. Once, while Rafe was at the wheel, and the girl was dozing with her coat over her face to shut out the fierce sun, Regis asked me, "What are the trailcities like?"

I tried to tell him, but I've never been good at boiling things down into descriptions, and when he found I was not disposed to talk, he fell silent and I was free to drowse over what I knew of the Trailmen and their world.

Nature seems to have a sameness on all inhabited worlds, tending toward the economy and simplicity of the human form. The upright carriage, freeing the hands, the opposable thumb, the color-sensitivity of retinal rods and cones, the development of language and of lengthy parental nurture—these things seem to be indispensable to the growth of civilization, and in the end they spell *human*. Except for minor variations depending on climate or footstuffs, the inhabitant of Megaera or Darkover is indistinguishable from the Terran or Sirian; differences are mainly cultural, and sometimes an isolated culture will mutate in a strange direction or remain atavists, somewhere halfway to the summit of the ladder of evolution—which, at least on the known planets, still reckons *homo sapiens* as the most complex of nature's forms.

The Trailmen were a pausing-place which had proved tenacious. When the mainstream of evolution on Darkover left the trees to struggle for existence on the ground, a few remained behind. Evolution did not cease for them, but evolved *homo arborens*: nocturnal, nyetalopic humanoids who live out their lives in the extensive forests.

The truck bumped over the bad, rutted roads. The wind was chilly. The truck, a mere conveyance for hauling, had no such refinements of luxury as windows. I jolted awake—what nonsense had I been thinking? Vague ideas about evolution swirled in my brain like burst bubbles—the Trailmen? They were just the Trailmen, who could explain them? Jay Allison, maybe? Rafe turned his head and asked, "Where do we pull up for the night? It's getting dark, and we have all this gear to sort!" I roused myself, and took over the business of the expedition again.

But when the trucks had been parked and a tent pitched and the pack animals unloaded and hobbled, and a start made at getting the gear together —when all this had been done I lay awake, listening to Kendricks' heavy snoring, but myself afraid to sleep. Dozing in the truck, an odd lapse of consciousness had come over me—myself yet not myself, drowsing over thoughts I did not recognize as my own. If I slept, who would I be when I woke?

We had made our camp in the bend of an enormous river, wide and shallow and unbridged—the river Kadarin, traditionally a point of no return for humans on Darkover. Beyond the river lay thick forests, and beyond the forests the slopes of the Hellers, rising upward and upward; and their every fold and every valley was filled to the brim with forest, and in the forests lived the Trailmen.

But though all this country was thickly populated with outlying colonies and nests, it would be no use to bargain with any of them; we must deal with the Old One of the North Nest, where I had spent so many of my boyhood years.

From time immemorial, the Trailmen—usually inoffensive—had kept strict boundaries marked between their lands and the lands of ground-dwelling men. They never came beyond the Kadarin. On the other hand, any human who ventured into their territory became, by that act, fair game for attack.

A few of the Darkovan mountain people had trade treaties with the Trailmen; they traded clothing, forged metals, small implements, in return for nuts, bark for dyestuffs and certain leaves and mosses for drugs. In return, the Trailmen permitted them to hunt in the forest lands without being molested. But other humans, venturing into Trailmen territory, ran the risk of merciless raiding; the Trailmen were not bloodthirsty, and did not kill for the sake of killing, but they attacked in packs of two or three dozen, and their prey would be stripped and plundered of everything portable.

Traveling through their country would be dangerous.

I sat in front of the tent, staring at the expanse of water, rippling pink in the sunrise. The pack animals cropped short grass behind the tent. The trucks were vast sphinxes, shrouded under tarpaulins glistening with early dew. Regis Hastur came out of the tent, rubbed his eyes and joined me at the water's edge.

"What do you think? Is it going to be a bad trip?"

"I wouldn't think so. I know the main trails and I can keep clear of them. It's only—" I hesitated, and Regis demanded, "What else?"

I said it, after a minute. "It's—well, it's you. If anything happens to you, we'll be held responsible to all Darkover."

He grinned. In the red sunlight he looked like a painting from some old legend. "Responsibility? You didn't strike me as the worrying type, Jason. What sort of duffer do you take me for? I know how to handle myself in the mountains, and I'm not afraid of the Trailmen, even if I don't know them as you do. Come on—shall I get breakfast or will you?"

I shrugged, busying myself near the fire. Somewhat to the surprise of the other Terrans—Kendricks and Rafe—Regis had done his share of the camp work at every halt; not ostentatiously either, but cheerfully and matter-of-factly. This surprised Rafe and Kendricks, who accepted the Terran custom of the higher echelons leaving such things to the buck privates. But in spite of their rigid caste distinctions, social differences of the Terran type simply don't exist on Darkover. Neither does gallantry, and only Kendricks objected when Kyla took on the job of seeing to the packloading and did her share of heaving boxes and crates.

After a while Regis joined me at the fire again. The three roughneck brothers had come out and were splashing noisily in the ford of the river. The

37

rest were still sleeping. Regis asked, "Shall I roust them out?"

"No need. The Kadarin's fed by ocean tides and we'll have to wait for low water to cross. Nearly noon before we could get across without ruining half our gear."

Regis sniffed at the kettle. "Sounds good," he decided, and dunked his bowl in; sat down, balancing the food on his knee. I followed suit, and Regis demanded, "Tell me something about yourself, Jason. Where did you learn so much about the Hellers? Lerrys was on the 'Narr campaign, but you don't seem old enough for that."

"I'm older than I look," I said, "but I wasn't old enough for that." (During the brief civil war when Darkovans fought Trailmen in the passes of 'Narr, I had—as a boy of eleven—spied on the human invaders; but I didn't tell Regis that.) "I lived with them for eight years."

"*Sharra!* Was that you?" The Darkovan prince looked genuinely impressed. "No wonder you got this assignment! Jason, I envy you!"

I gave a short bark of laughter.

"No, I'm serious, Jason. As a boy I tried to get into the Terran space service. But my family finally convinced me that as a Hastur I had my work already cut out for me—that we Hasturs were committed to trying to keep Terra and Darkover on a peaceful basis. It puts me at a terrific disadvantage, you know. They all think I ought to be wearing cushions around my head in case I take a tumble."

I snapped, "Then why in hell did they let you come on a dangerous mission like this?"

The Hastur's eyes twinkled, but his face was completely deadpan and his voice grave. "I pointed out to my grandsire that I have been assiduous in my duty to the Hasturs. I have five sons, three legitimate, born in the past two years."

I choked, spluttered and exploded into laughter as Regis got to his feet and went to rinse his bowl in the river.

The sun was high before we left the camp. While the others were packing up the last oddments, ready for the saddle, I gave Kyla the task of readying the rucksacks we'd carry after the trails got too bad even for the pack animals, and went to stand at the water's edge, checking the depth of the ford and glancing up at the smoke-hazed rifts between peak and peak.

The men were packing up the small tent we'd use in the forests, moving around with a good deal of horseplay and a certain brisk bustle. They were a good crew, I'd already discovered. Rafe and Lerrys and the three Darkovan brothers were tireless, cheerful, and mountain-hardened. Kendricks, obviously out of his element, could be implicitly relied on to follow orders, and I felt that I could fall back on him. Strange as it seemed, the very fact that he was a Terran was vaguely comforting, where I'd anticipated it would be a nuisance.

The girl Kyla was still something of an unknown quantity. She was too taut and quiet, working her share but seldom contributing a word—we were not yet in mountain country. So far she was quiet and touchy with me, although she seemed natural enough with the Darkovans, and I let her alone.

"Hi, Jason, get a move on," someone shouted, and I walked back toward the clearing, squinting in the sun. It hurt, and I touched my face gingerly, suddenly realizing what had happened. Yesterday, riding in the uncovered truck, and this morning, unused to the fierce sun of these latitudes, I had neglected to take the proper precautions against exposure and my face was reddening with sunburn. I walked toward Kyla, who was cinching a final load on one of the pack animals, which she did efficiently enough.

She didn't wait for me to ask, but sized up the situation with one amused glance at my face. "Sunburn? Put some of this on it." She produced a tube of white stuff; I twisted at the top inexpertly, and she took it from me, squeezed the stuff out in her palm and said, "Stand still and bend down your head."

She smeared the mixture across my forehead and cheeks. It felt cold and good. I started to thank her, then broke off as she burst out laughing. "What's the matter?"

"You should see yourself!" she gurgled.

I wasn't amused. No doubt I presented a grotesque appearance, and no doubt she had the right to laugh at it, but I scowled. It hurt. Intending to put things back on the proper footing, I demanded, "Did you make up the climbing loads?"

"All except bedding. I wasn't sure how much to allow," she said. "Jason, have you eyeshades for when you get on snow?" I nodded, and she instructed severely, "Don't forget them. Snowblindness—I give you my word—is even more unpleasant than sunburn—and *very* painful!"

"Damn it, girl, I'm not stupid!" I exploded.

She said, in her expressionless monotone again, "Then you *ought* to have known better than to get sunburnt. Here, put this in your pocket," she handed me the tube of sunburn cream. "Maybe I'd better check up on some of the others and make sure they haven't forgotten." She went off without a word, leaving me with an unpleasant feeling that she'd come off best, that she considered me an irresponsible scamp.

Forth had said almost the same thing.

I told the Darkovan brothers to urge the pack animals across the narrowest part of the ford, and gestured to Lerrys and Kyla to ride one on either side of Kendricks, who might not be aware of the swirling, treacherous currents of a mountain river. Rafe could not urge his edgy horse into the water; he finally dismounted, took off his boots, and led the creature across the slippery rocks. I crossed last, riding close to Regis Hastur, alert for dangers and thinking resentfully that anyone so important to Darkover's policies should not be risked on such a mission. Why, if the Terran Legate had (unthinkably!) come with us, he would be surrounded by bodyguards, Secret Service men and dozens of precautions against accident, assassination or misadventure.

All that day we rode upward, encamping at the furthest point we could travel with pack animals or mounted. The next day's climb would enter the dangerous trails we must travel afoot. We pitched a comfortable camp, but I admit I slept badly. Kendricks and Lerrys and Rafe had blinding headaches from the sun and the thinness of the air; I was more used to these conditions, but I felt a sense of unpleasant pressure, and my ears rang. Regis arrogantly denied any discomfort, but he moaned and cried out continuously in his sleep until Lerrys kicked him, after which he was silent and, I feared, sleepless. Kyla seemed the least affected of any; probably she had been at higher altitudes more continuously than any of us. But there were dark circles beneath her eyes.

However, no one complained as we readied ourselves for the last long climb upward. If we were fortunate, we could cross Dammerung before nightfall; at the very least, we should bivouac tonight very near the pass. Our camp had been made at the last level spot; we partially hobbled the pack animals so they would not stray too far, and left ample food for them, and cached all but the most necessary of light trail gear. As we prepared to start upward on the steep, narrow track—hardly more than a rabbit-run—I glanced at Kyla and stated, "We'll work on rope from the first stretch. Starting now."

One of the Darkovan brothers stared at me with contempt. "Call yourself a mountain man, Jason? Why, my little daughter could scramble up *that* track without so much as a push on her behind!"

I set my chin and glared at him. "The rocks aren't easy, and some of these men aren't used to working on rope at all. We might as well get used to it, because when we start working along the ledges, I don't want anybody who doesn't know how."

They still didn't like it, but nobody protested further until I directed the huge Kendricks to the center of the second rope. He glared viciously at the light nylon line and demanded with some apprehension, "Hadn't I better go last until I know what I'm doing? Hemmed in between the two of you, I'm apt to do something damned dumb!"

Hjalmar roared with laughter and informed him that the center place on a three-man rope was always reserved for weaklings, novices and amateurs.

I expected Kendricks' temper to flare up; the burly Spaceforce man and the Darkovan giant glared at one another, then Kendricks only shrugged and knotted the line through his belt. Kyla warned Kendricks and Lerrys about looking down from ledges, and we started.

The first stretch was almost too simple, a clear track winding higher and higher for a couple of miles. Pausing to rest for a moment, we could turn and see the entire valley outspread below us. Gradually the trail grew steeper, in spots pitched almost at a 50-degree angle, and was scattered with gravel, loose rock and shale, so that we placed our feet carefully, leaning forward to catch at handholds and steady ourselves against rocks. I tested each boulder carefully, since any weight placed against an unsteady rock might dislodge it on somebody below. One of the Darkovan brothers—Vardo, I thought—was behind me, separated by ten or twelve feet of slack rope, and twice when his feet slipped on gravel he stumbled and gave me an unpleasant jerk. What he muttered was perfectly true; on slopes like this, where a fall wasn't dangerous anyhow, it was better to work unroped; then a slip bothered no one but the slipper. But I was finding out what I wanted to know—what kind of climbers I had to lead through the Hellers.

Along a cliff face the trail narrowed horizontally, leading across a foot-wide ledge overhanging a sheer drop of fifty feet and covered with loose shale and scrub plants. Nothing, of course, to an experienced climber—a foot-wide ledge might as well be a four-lane superhighway. Kendricks made a nervous joke about a tightrope walker, but when his turn came he picked his way securely, without losing bal-

ance. The amateurs—Lerrys Ridenow, Regis, Rafe—
came across without hesitation, but I wondered how
well they would have done at a less secure altitude;
to a real mountaineer, a footpath is a footpath,
whether in a meadow, above a two-foot drop, a thirty-foot ledge, or a sheer mountain face three miles
above the first level spot.

After crossing the ledge, the going was harder. A
steeper trail, in places nearly imperceptible, led between thick scrub and overhanging trees, closely
clustered. In spots their twisted roots obscured the
trail; in others the persistent growth had thrust aside
rocks and dirt. We had to make our way through
tangles of underbrush which would have been nothing to a Trailman, but which made our ground-
accustomed bodies ache with the effort of getting
over or through them; and once the track was totally
blocked by a barricade of tangled dead brushwood,
borne down on floodwater after a sudden thaw or
cloudburst. We had to work painfully around it over
a three-hundred-foot rockslide, which we could cross
only one at a time, crab-fashion, leaning double to
balance ourselves; and no one complained now
about the rope.

Toward noon I had the first intimation that we
were not alone on the slope.

At first it was no more than a glimpse of motion
out of the corner of my eyes, the shadow of a
shadow. The fourth time I saw it, I called softly to
Kyla, "See anything?"

"I was beginning to think it was my eyes, or the
altitude. I saw, Jason."

"Look for a spot where we can take a break," I
directed. We climbed along a shallow ledge, the
faint imperceptible flutters in the brushwood climb-

44

ing with us on either side. I muttered to the girl, "I'll be glad when we get clear of this. At least we'll be able to see what's coming after us!"

"If it comes to a fight," she said surprisingly, "I'd rather fight on gravel than ice."

Over a rise, there was a roaring sound. Kyla swung up and balanced on a rock-wedged tree root, cupped her mouth to her hands, and called, "Rapids!"

I pulled myself up to the edge of the drop and stood looking down into the narrow gully. Here the track we had been following was crossed and obscured by the deep, roaring rapids of a mountain stream.

Less than twenty feet across, it tumbled in an icy flood, almost a waterfall, pitching over the lip of a crag above us. It had sliced a ravine five feet deep in the mountainside, and came roaring down with a rushing noise that made my head vibrate. It looked formidable; anyone stepping into it would be knocked off his feet in seconds, and swept a thousand feet down the mountainside by the force of the current.

Rafe scrambled gingerly over the gullied lip of the channel it had cut, and bent carefully to scoop up water in his palm and drink. "Phew, it's colder than Zandru's ninth hell. Must come straight down from a glacier!"

It did. I remembered the trail and remembered the spot. Kendricks joined me at the water's edge, and asked, "How do we get across?"

"I'm not sure," I said, studying the racing white torrent. Overhead, about twenty feet from where we clustered on the slope, the thick branches of enormous trees overhung the rapids, their long roots partially bared, gnarled and twisted by recurrent floods; and between these trees swayed one of the queer swing-bridges of the Trailmen, hanging only about ten feet above the water.

Even I had never learned to navigate one of these swinging bridges without assistance; human arms are no longer suited to brachiation. I might have managed it once; but at present, except as a desperate final expedient, it was out of the question. Rafe or Lerrys, who were lightly built and acrobatic, could probably do it as a simple stunt on the level, in a field; on a steep and rocky mountainside, where a fall might mean being dashed a thousand feet down the torrent, I doubted it. The Trailmen's bridge was out—but what other choice was there?

I beckoned to Kendricks, he being the man I was the most inclined to trust with my life at the moment, and said, "It looks uncrossable, but I think two men could get across, if they were steady on their feet. The others can hold us on ropes, in case we do get knocked down. If we can get to the opposite bank, we can stretch a fixed rope from that snub of rock—" I pointed, "and the others can cross with that. The first men over will be the only ones to run any risk. Want to try?"

I liked it better that he didn't answer right away, but went to the edge of the gully and peered down the rocky chasm. Doubtless, if we were knocked down, all seven of the others could haul us up again; but not before we'd been badly smashed on the rocks. And once again I caught that elusive shadow of movement in the brushwood; if the Trailmen chose a moment when we were half-in, half-out of the rapids, we'd be ridiculously vulnerable to attack.

"We ought to be able to get a fixed rope easier than that," Hjalmar said, and took one of the spares from his rucksack. He coiled it, making a running loop on one end, and, standing precariously on the lip of the rapids, sent it spinning toward the outcrop of rock we had chosen as a fixed point. "If I can get it over—"

The rope fell short, and Hjalmar reeled it in and cast the loop again. He made three more unsuccessful tries before finally, with held breath, we watched the noose settle over the rocky snub. Gently, pulling the line taut, we watched it stretch above the rapids. The knot tightened, fastened. Hjalmar grinned and let out his breath.

"There," he said, and jerked hard on the rope, testing it with a long hard pull. The rocky outcrop broke, with a sharp *crack*, split, and toppled entire into the rapids, the sudden jerk almost pulling Hjalmar off his feet. The boulder rolled, with a great bouncing splash, faster and faster down the mountain, taking the rope with it.

We just stood and stared for a minute. Hjalmar swore horribly, in the unprintable filth of the mountain tongue, and his brothers joined in. "How the devil was I to know the *rock* would split off?"

"Better for it to split now than when we were depending on it," Kyla said stolidly. "I have a better idea." She was untying herself from the rope as she spoke, and knotting one of the spares through her belt. She handed the other end of the rope to Lerrys. "Hold on to this," she said, and slipped out of her blanket windbreak, standing shivering in a thin sweater. She unstrapped her boots and tossed them to me. "Now boost me on your shoulders, Hjalmar."

Too late, I guessed her intention and shouted, "No, don't try—" But she had already clambered to an unsteady perch on the big Darkovan's shoulders and made a flying grab for the lowest loop of the trailmen's bridge. She hung there, swaying slightly and sickeningly, as the loose lianas gave to her weight.

"Hjalmar—Lerrys—haul her down!"

"I'm lighter than any of you," Kyla called shrilly, "and not hefty enough to be any use on the ropes!" Her voice quavered somewhat as she added, "—and hang on to that rope, Lerrys! If you lose it, I'll have done this for nothing!"

She gripped the loop of vine and reached, with her free hand, for the next loop. Now she was swinging out over the edge of the boiling rapids. Tight-mouthed, I gestured to the others to spread out slightly below—not that anything would help her if she fell.

Hjalmar, watching as the woman gained the third loop, which joggled horribly to her slight weight, shouted suddenly, "Kyla, quick! The loop *beyond*— don't touch the next one! It's frayed—rotted through!"

Kyla brought her left hand up to her right on the third loop. She made a long reach, missed her grab, swung again, and clung, breathing hard, to the safe fifth loop. I watched, sick with dread. The damned girl should have told me what she intended.

Kyla glanced down and we got a glimpse of her face, glistening with the mixture of sunburn cream and sweat, drawn with effort. Her tiny swaying figure hung twelve feet above the white tumbling water, and if she lost her grip, only a miracle could bring her out alive. She hung there for a minute, jiggling slightly, then started a long back-and-forward swing. On the third forward swing she made a long leap and grabbed at the final loop.

It slipped through her fingers; she made a wild grab with the other hand, and the liana dipped sharply under her weight, raced through her fingers, and, with a sharp snap, broke in two. She gave a wild shriek as it parted, and twisted her body frantically in mid-air, landing asprawl half-in, half-out of the rapids, but on the further bank. She hauled her legs up on dry land and crouched there, drenched to the waist but safe.

The Darkovans were yelling in delight. I motioned to Lerrys to make his end of the rope fast around a hefty tree-root, and shouted, "Are you hurt?" She indicated in pantomime that the thundering of the water drowned words, and bent to secure her end of the rope. In sign language I gestured to her to make very sure of the knots; if anyone slipped, she hadn't the weight to hold us.

I hauled on the rope myself to test it, and it held fast. I slung her boots around my neck by their cords, then, gripping the fixed rope, Kendricks and I stepped into the water.

It was even icier than I expected, and my first step was nearly the last; the rush of the white water knocked me to my knees, and I floundered and would have measured my length except for my hands on the fixed rope. Buck Kendricks grabbed at me, letting go the rope to do it, and I swore at him, raging, while we got on our feet again and braced ourselves against the onrushing current.

While we struggled in the pounding waters, I admitted to myself that we could never have crossed without the rope Kyla had risked her life to fix.

Shivering, we got across and hauled ourselves out. I signaled to the others to cross two at a time, and Kyla seized my elbow. "Jason—"

"Later, dammit!" I had to shout to make myself heard over the roaring water, as I held out a hand to help Rafe get his footing on the ledge.

"This—can't—wait," she yelled, cupping her hands and shouting into my ear. I turned on her. "*What!*"

"There are—*Trailmen*—on the top level—of that bridge! I saw them! They cut the loop!"

Regis and Hjalmar came struggling across last; Regis, lightly-built, was swept off his feet and Hjalmar turned to grab him, but I shouted to him to keep clear—they were still roped together and if the ropes fouled we might drown someone. Lerrys and I leaped down and hauled Regis clear; he coughed, spitting icy water, drenched to the skin.

I motioned to Lerrys to leave the fixed rope, though I had little hope that it would be there when we returned, and looked quickly around, debating what to do. Regis and Rafe and I were wet clear through; the others were wet to well above the knee. At this altitude, this was dangerous, although we were not yet high enough to worry about frostbite. Trailmen or no Trailmen, we must run the lesser risk of finding a place where we could kindle a fire and dry out.

"Up there—there's a clearing," I said briefly, and hurried them along.

It was hard climbing now, on rock, and there were places where we had to scrabble for handholds, and flatten ourselves out against an almost sheer wall. The keen wind rose as we climbed higher, whining through the thick forest, soughing in the rocky outcrops, and biting through our soaked clothing with icy teeth. Kendricks was having hard going now, and I helped him as much as I could, but I was aching with cold. We gained the clearing, a small bare spot on a lesser peak, and I directed the two Darkovan brothers, who were the driest, to gather dry brushwood and get a fire going. It was hardly near enough to sunset to camp. But by the time we were dry enough to go on safely, it would be, so I gave orders to get the tent up, then rounded angrily on Kyla:

"See here, another time don't try any dangerous tricks unless you're ordered to!"

"Go easy on her," Regis Hastur interceded, "we'd never have crossed without the fixed rope. Good work, girl."

"You keep out of this!" I snapped. It was true, yet resentment boiled in me as Kyla's plain sullen face glowed under the praise from Hastur.

The fact was—I admitted it grudgingly—a lightweight like Kyla ran less risk on an acrobat's bridge than in that kind of roaring current. That did not lessen my annoyance; and Regis Hastur's interference, and the foolish grin on the girl's face, made me boil over.

I wanted to question her further about the sight of Trailmen on the bridge, but decided against it. We had been spared attack on the rapids, so it wasn't impossible that a group, not hostile, was simply watching our progress—maybe even aware that we were on a peaceful mission.

But I didn't believe it for a minute. If I knew anything about the Trailmen, it was this—one could not judge them by human standards at all. I tried to decide what I would have done, as a Trailman, but my brain wouldn't run that way at the moment.

The Darkovan brothers had built up the fire with a thoroughly reckless disregard of watching eyes. It seemed to me that the morale and fitness of the shivering crew was of more value at the moment than caution; and around the roaring fire, feeling my soaked clothes warming to the blaze and drinking boiling hot tea from a mug, it seemed that we were right. Optimism reappeared. Kyla, letting Hjalmar dress her hands which had been rubbed raw by the slipping lianas, made jokes with the men about her feat of acrobatics.

We had made camp on the summit of an outlying arm of the main ridge of the Hellers, and the whole massive range lay before our eyes, turned to a million colors in the declining sun. Green and turquoise and rose, the mountains were even more beautiful than I remembered. The shoulder of the high slope we had just climbed had obscured the real mountain *massif* from our sight, and I saw Kendricks' eyes widen as he realized that this high summit we had just mastered was only the first step of the task which lay before us. The real ridge rose ahead, thickly forested on the lower slopes, then strewn with rock and granite like the landscape of an airless, deserted moon. And above the rock, there were straight walls capped with blinding snow and ice. Down one peak a glacier flowed, a waterfall, a cascade shockingly arrested in motion. I murmured the Trailmen's name for the mountain, aloud, and translated it for the others:

"The Wall around the World."

"Good name for it," Lerrys murmured, coming

with his mug in his hand to look at the mountain. "Jason, the big peak there has never been climbed, has it?"

"I can't remember." My teeth were chattering and I went back toward the fire. Regis surveyed the distant glacier and murmured, "It doesn't look too bad. There could be a route along that western *arête*—Hjalmar, weren't you with the expedition that climbed and mapped High Kimbi?"

The giant nodded, rather proudly. "We got within a hundred feet of the top, then a snowstorm came up and we had to turn back. Some day we'll tackle the Wall around the World—it's been tried, but no one ever climbed the peak."

"No one ever will," Lerrys stated positively, "There's two hundred feet of sheer rock cliff. Prince Regis, you'd need wings to get up. And there's the avalanche ledge they call Hell's Alley—"

Kendricks broke in irritably, "I don't care whether it's ever been climbed or ever will be climbed, we're not going to climb it now!" He stared at me and added, "I hope!"

"We're not." I was glad of the interruption. If the youngsters and amateurs wanted to amuse themselves plotting hypothetical attacks on unclimbable sierras, that was all very well, but it was, if nothing worse, a great waste of time. I showed Kendricks a notch in the ridge, thousands of feet lower than the peaks, and well sheltered from the ice falls on either side.

"That's Dammerung; we're going through there. We won't be on the mountain at all, and it's less than 22,000 feet high in the pass—although there are some bad ledges and washes. We'll keep clear of the main tree-roads if we can, and all the mapped

Trailmen's villages, but we may run into wandering bands—" abruptly I made my decision and gestured them around me.

"From this point," I broke the news, "we're liable to be attacked. Kyla, tell them what you saw."

She put down her mug. Her face was serious again, as she related what she had seen on the bridge. "We're on a peaceful mission, but they don't know that yet. The thing to remember is that they do not wish to kill, only to wound and rob. If we show fight—" she displayed a short ugly knife, which she tucked matter-of-factly into her shirt-front, "they will run away again."

Lerrys loosened a narrow dagger which, until this moment, I had thought purely ornamental. He said, "Mind if I say something more, Jason? I remember from the 'Narr campaign—the Trailmen fight at close quarters, and by human standards they fight dirty." He looked around fiercely, his unshaven face glinting as he grinned. "One more thing. I like elbow room. Do we have to stay roped together when we start out again?"

I thought it over. His enthusiasm for a fight made me feel both annoyed and curiously delighted. "I won't make anyone stay roped who thinks he'd be safer without it," I said. "We'll decide that when the time comes, anyway. But personally—the Trailmen are used to running along narrow ledges, and we're not. Their first tactic would probably be to push us off, one by one. If we're roped, we can fend them off better." I dismissed the subject, adding, "Just now, the important thing is to dry out."

Kendricks remained at my side after the others had gathered around the fire, looking into the thick forest which sloped up to our campsite. He said,

"This place looks as if it had been used for a camp before. Aren't we just as vulnerable to attack here as we would be anywhere else?"

He had hit on the one thing I hadn't wanted to talk about. This clearing was altogether too convenient. I only said, "At least there aren't so many ledges to push us off."

Kendricks muttered, "You've got the only blaster!"

"I left it at Carthon," I said truthfully. Then I laid down the law:

"Listen, Buck. If we kill a single Trailman, except in hand-to-hand fight in self-defense, we might as well pack up and go home. We're on a peaceful mission, and we're begging a favor. Even if we're attacked—we kill only as a last resort, and in hand-to-hand combat!"

"Damned primitive frontier planet—"

"Would you rather die of the Trailmen's disease?"

He said savagely, "We're apt to catch it anyway —here. You're immune, you don't care, you're safe! The rest of us are on a suicide mission—and damn it, when I die I want to take a few of those goddam monkeys with me!"

I bent my head, bit my lip and said nothing. Buck couldn't be blamed for the way he felt. After a moment, I pointed to the notch in the ridge again. "It's not so far. Once we get through Dammerung, it's easy going into the Trailmen's city. Beyond there, it's all civilized."

"Maybe *you* call it civilization," Kendricks said, and turned away.

"Come on, let's finish drying our feet."

And at that moment they hit us.

CHAPTER V

KENDRICKS' YELL was the only warning I had before
I was fighting away something scrabbling up my
back. I whirled and ripped the creature away, and
saw dimly that the clearing was filled to the rim
with an explosion of furry white bodies. I cupped
my hands and yelled, in the only Trailman dialect
I knew, "Hold off! We come in peace!"

One of them yelled something unintelligible and
plunged at me—another tribe! I saw a white-furred,
chinless face, contorted in rage, a small ugly knife
—a female! I ripped out my own knife, fending away
a savage slash. Something tore white-hot across the
knuckles of my hand; the fingers went limp and my
knife fell, and the Trailman woman snatched it up
and made off with her prize, swinging lithely upward into the treetops.

I searched quickly, gripped with my good hand
at the bleeding knuckles, and found Regis Hastur
struggling at the edge of a ledge with a pair of the
creatures. The crazy thought ran through my mind
that if they killed him all Darkover would rise and
exterminate the Trailmen and it would all be my
fault. Then Regis tore one hand free, and made a
curious motion with his fingers.

It looked like an immense green spark a foot long,
or like a fireball. It exploded in one creature's white
face and she gave a wild howl of terror and anguish,
scrabbled blindly at her eyes, and with a despair-
ing shriek, ran for the shelter of the trees. The pack
of Trailmen gave a long formless wail, and then

they were gathering, flying, retreating into the shadows. Rafe yelled something obscene and then a bolt of bluish flame lanced toward the retreating pack. One of the humanoids fell without a cry, pitching senseless over the ledge.

I ran toward Rafe, struggling with him for the shocker he had drawn from its hiding place inside his shirt. "You blind damned fool!" I cursed him. "You may have ruined everything—"

"They'd have killed him without it," he retorted wrathfully. He had evidently failed to see how efficiently Regis defended himself. Rafe motioned toward the fleeing pack and sneered, "Why don't you go with your friends?"

With a grip I thought I had forgotten, I got my hand around Rafe's knuckles and squeezed. His hand went limp and I snatched the shocker and pitched it over the ledge.

"One word and I'll pitch you after it," I warned. "Who's hurt?"

Garin was blinking senselessly, half dazed by a blow; Regis' forehead had been gashed and dripped blood, and Hjalmar's thigh sliced in a clean cut. My own knuckles were laid bare and the hand was getting numb. It was a little while before anybody noticed Kyla, crouched over speechless with pain. She reeled and turned deathly white when we touched her; we stretched her out where she was, and got her shirt off, and Kendricks crowded up beside us to examine the wound.

"A clean cut," he said, but I didn't hear. Something had turned over inside me, like a hand stirring up my brain, and . . .

Jay Allison looked around with a gasp of sudden

vertigo. He was not in Forth's office, but standing precariously near the edge of a cliff. He shut his eyes briefly, wondering if he were having one of his worst nightmares, and opened them on a familiar face.

Buck Kendricks was bone-white, his mouth widening as he said hoarsely, "Jay! Doctor Allison —for God's sake—"

A doctor's training creates reactions that are almost reflexes; Jay Allison recovered some degree of sanity as he became aware that someone was stretched out in front of him, half naked, and bleeding profusely. He motioned away the crowding strangers and said in his bad Darkovan, "Let her alone, this is my work." He didn't know enough words to curse them away, so he switched to Terran, speaking to Kendricks:

"Buck, get these people away, give the patient some air. Where's my surgical case?" He bent and probed briefly, realizing only now that the injured was a woman, and young.

The wound was only a superficial laceration; whatever sharp instrument had inflicted it, had turned on the costal bone without penetrating lung tissue. It could have been sutured, but Kendricks handed him only a badly-filled first-aid kit; so Dr. Allison covered it tightly with a plastic clipshield which would seal it from further bleeding, and let it alone. By the time he had finished, the strange girl had begun to stir. She said haltingly, "Jason—?"

"Dr. Allison," he corrected tersely, surprised in a minor way—the major surprise had blurred lesser ones—that she knew his name. Kendricks spoke swiftly to the girl, in one of the Darkovan languages Jay didn't understand, and then drew Jay aside, out of earshot. He said in a shaken voice, "Jay, I didn't know—I wouldn't have believed—you're *Doctor Allison?* Good God—Jason!"

And then he moved fast. "What's the matter? Oh, Christ, Jay, don't faint on me!"

Jay was aware that he didn't come out of it too bravely, but anyone who blamed him (he thought resentfully) should try it on for size; going to sleep in a comfortably closed-in office and waking up on a cliff at the outer edges of nowhere. His hand hurt; he saw that it was bleeding and flexed it experimentally, trying to determine that no tendons had been injured. He rapped, "How did this happen?"

"Sir, keep your voice down—or speak Darkovan!"

Jay blinked again. Kendricks was still the only familiar thing in a strangely vertiginous universe. The Spaceforce man said huskily, "Before God, Jay, I hadn't any idea—and I've known you how long? Eight, nine years?"

Jay said, "That idiot Forth!" and swore, the colorless profanity of an indoor man.

Somebody shouted, "Jason!" in an imperative voice, and Kendricks said shakily, "Jay, if they see you—you literally are not the same man!"

"Obviously not." Jay looked at the tent, one pole still unpitched. "Anyone in there?"

"Not yet." Kendricks almost shoved him inside. "I'll tell them—I'll tell them something." He took a radiant from his pocket, set it down and stared at Allison in the flickering light, and said something profane. "You'll—you'll be all right here?"

Jay nodded. It was all he could manage. He was keeping a tight hold on his nerves; if it went, he'd start to rave like a madman. A little time passed, there were strange noises outside, and then there was a polite cough and a man walked into the tent.

He was obviously a Darkovan aristocrat and looked vaguely familiar, though Jay had no conscious memory of seeing him before. Tall and slender, he possessed that perfect and exquisite masculine beauty sometimes seen among Darkovans, and he spoke to Jay familiarly but with surprising courtesy:

"I have told them you are not to be disturbed for a moment, that your hand is worse than we believed. A surgeon's hands are delicate things, Doctor Allison, and I hope that yours are not badly injured. Will you let me look?"

Jay Allison drew back his hand automatically, then, conscious of the churlishness of the gesture, let the stranger take it in his and look at the fingers. The man said, "It does not seem serious. I was sure it was something more than that." He raised grave eyes. "You don't even remember my name, do you, Dr. Allison?"

"You know who I am?"

"Dr. Forth didn't tell me. But we Hasturs are partly telepathic, Jason—forgive me—Doctor Allison. I have known from the first that you were possessed by a god or daemon."

"Superstitious rubbish," Jay snapped. "Typical of a Darkovan!"

"It is a convenient manner of speaking, no more," said the young Hastur, overlooking the rudeness. "I suppose I could learn your terminology, if I considered it worth the effort. I have had psi training, and I can tell the difference when half of a man's soul has driven out the other half. Perhaps I can restore you to yourself—"

"If you think I'd have some Darkovan freak meddling with my mind—" Jay began hotly, then stopped. Under Regis' grave eyes, he felt a surge of unfamiliar humility. This crew of men needed their leader, and obviously he, Jay Allison, wasn't the leader they needed. He covered his eyes with one hand.

Regis bent and put a hand on his shoulder, compassionately, but Jay twitched it off, and his voice, when he found it, was bitter and defensive and cold.

"All right. The work's the thing. I can't do it, Jason can. You're a parapsych. If you can switch me off—go right ahead!"

I stared at Regis, passing a hand across my forehead. "What happened?" I demanded, and in even swifter apprehension, "Where's Kyla? She was hurt—"

"Kyla's all right," Regis said, but I got up quickly to make sure. Kyla was outside, lying quite comfortably on a roll of blankets. She was propped up on her elbow drinking something hot, and there was a good smell of hot food in the air. I stared at Regis and demanded, "I didn't conk out, did I, from a little scratch like this?" I looked carelessly at my gashed hand.

"Wait—" Regis held me back, "don't go out just yet. Do you remember what happened, Doctor Allison?"

I stared in growing horror, my worst fear confirmed. Regis said quietly, "You—changed. Probably from the shock of seeing—" he stopped in mid-sentence, and I said, "The last thing I remember is seeing that Kyla was bleeding, when we got her clothes off. But—good Gods, a little blood wouldn't scare *me*, and Jay Allison's a surgeon, would it bring him roaring up like that?"

"I couldn't say." Regis looked as if he knew more than he was telling. "I don't believe that Dr. Allison —he's not much like you—was very concerned with Kyla. Are you?"

"Damn right I am. I want to make sure she's all right—" I stopped abruptly. "Regis—did they all see it?"

"Only Kendricks and I," Regis said, "and we will not speak of it."

I said, "Thanks," and felt his reassuring hand-clap. Damn it, demigod or prince, I *liked* Regis.

I went out and accepted some food from the kettle and sat down between Kyla and Kendricks to eat. I was shaken, weak with reaction. Furthermore, I realized that we couldn't stay here. It was too vulnerable to attack. So, in our present condition, were we. If we could push on hard enough to get near Dammerung Pass tonight, then tomorrow we could cross it early, before the sun warmed the snow and we had snowslides and slush to deal with. Beyond Dammerung, I knew the tribesmen and could speak their language.

I mentioned this, and Kendricks looked doubtfully at Kyla. "Can she climb?"

"Can she stay here?" I countered. But I went and sat beside her anyhow:

"How badly are you hurt? Do you think you can travel?"

She said fiercely, "Of course I can climb! I tell you, I'm no weak girl, I'm a free Amazon!" She flung off the blanket somebody had tucked around her legs. Her lips looked a little pinched, but the long stride was steady as she walked to the fire and demanded more soup.

We struck the camp in minutes. The Trailmen

band of raiding females had snatched up almost everything portable, and there was no sense in striking and catching the tent; they'd return and hunt it out. If we came back with a Trailman escort, we wouldn't need it anyway. I ordered them to leave everything but the lightest gear, and examined each remaining rucksack. Rations for the night we would spend in the pass, our few remaining blankets, ropes, sunglasses. Everything else I ruthlessly ordered left behind.

It was harder going now. For one thing, the sun was lowering, and the evening wind was icy. Nearly every one of us had some hurt, slight in itself, which hindered us in climbing. Kyla was white and rigid, but did not spare herself; Kendricks was suffering from mountain sickness at this altitude, and I gave him all the help I could, but with my stiffening slashed hand I wasn't having too easy a time myself.

There was one expanse that was sheer rock-climbing, flattened like bugs against a wall, scrabbling for handholds and footholds. I felt it a point of pride to lead, and I led; but by the time we had climbed the thirty-foot wall, and scrambled along a ledge to where we could pick up the trail again, I was ready to give over. Crowding together on the ledge, I changed places with the veteran Lerrys, who was better than most professional climbers.

He muttered, "I thought you said this was a *trail!*"

I stretched my mouth in what was supposed to be a grin and didn't quite make it. "For the Trailmen, this is a super-highway. And no one else ever comes this way."

Now we climbed slowly over snow; once or twice we had to flounder through drifts, and once a brief bitter snowstorm blotted out sight for twenty minutes, while we hugged each other on the ledge, clinging wildly against wind and icy sleet.

We bivouacked that night in a crevasse blown almost clean of snow, well above the tree-line, where only scrubby unkillable thornbushes clustered. We tore down some of them and piled them up as a windbreak, and bedded beneath it; but we all thought with aching regret of the comfort of the camp gear we'd abandoned.

That night remains in my mind as one of the most miserable in memory. Except for the slight ringing in my ears, the height alone did not bother me, but the others did not fare so well. Most of the men had blinding headaches, Kyla's slashed side must have given her considerable pain, and Kendricks had succumbed to mountain-sickness in its most agonizing form: severe cramps and vomiting. I was desperately uneasy about all of them, but there was nothing I could do; the only cure for mountain-sickness is oxygen or a lower altitude, neither of which was practical.

In the windbreak we doubled up, sharing blankets and body warmth. I took a last look around the close space before crawling in beside Kendricks, and saw the girl bedding down slightly apart from the others. I started to say something, but Kendricks spoke first.

"Better crawl in with us, girl." He added, coldly but not unkindly, "You needn't worry about any funny stuff."

Kyla gave me just the flicker of a grin, and I realized she was including me on the Darkovan side of a joke against this big man who was so unaware of Darkovan etiquette. But her voice was cool and

64

curt as she said, "I'm not worrying," and loosened her heavy coat slightly before creeping into the nest of blankets between us.

It was painfully cramped, and chilly in spite of the self-heating blankets; we crowded close together and Kyla's head rested on my shoulder. I felt her snuggle closely to me, half asleep, hunting for a warm place; and I found myself very much aware of her closeness, curiously grateful to her. An ordinary woman would have protested, if only as a matter of form, to sharing blankets with two strange men. I realized that if Kyla had refused to crawl in with us, she would have called attention to her sex much *more* than she did by matter-of-factly behaving as if she were male.

She shivered convulsively, and I whispered, "Side hurting? Are you cold?"

"A little. It's been a long time since I've been at these altitudes, too. What it really is—I can't get those women out of my head."

Kendricks coughed, moving uncomfortably. "I don't understand—those creatures who attacked us —all women—?"

I explained briefly. "Among the People of the Sky, as everywhere, more females are born than males. But the Trailmen's lives are so balanced that they have no room for extra females within the Nests— the cities. So when a girl child of the Sky People reaches womanhood, the other women drive her out of the city with kicks and blows, and she has to wander in the forest until some male comes after her and claims her and brings her back as his own. Then she can never be driven forth again, although if she bears no children she can be forced to be a servant to his other wives."

Kendricks made a little sound of disgust.

"You think it cruel," Kyla said with sudden passion, "but in the forest they can live and find their own food; they will not starve or die. Many of them prefer the forest life to living in the Nests, and they will fight away any male who comes near them. We who call ourselves human often make less provision for our spare women."

She was silent, sighing as if with pain. Kendricks made no reply except for a non-committal grunt. I held myself back by main force from touching Kyla, remembering what she was, and finally said, "We'd better quit talking. The others want to sleep, if we don't."

After a time I heard Kendricks snoring, and Kyla's quiet even breaths. I wondered drowsily how Jay would have felt about this situation—he who hated Darkover and avoided contact with every other human being, crowded between a Darkovan free Amazon and half a dozen assorted roughnecks. I turned the thought off, fearing it might somehow rearouse him in his brain.

But I had to think of something, anything to turn aside this consciousness of the woman's head against my chest, her warm breath coming and going against my bare neck. Only by the severest possible act of will did I keep myself from slipping my hand over her breasts, warm and palpable through the thin sweater. I wondered why Forth had called me undisciplined. I couldn't risk my leadership by making advances to our contracted guide—woman, Amazon or whatever.

Somehow the girl seemed to be the pivot point of all my thoughts. She was not part of the Terran HQ, she was not part of any world Jay Allison might have known. She belonged wholly to Jason, to *my* world. Between sleep and waking, I lost myself in a dream of skimming flight-wise along the tree-roads, chasing the distant form of a girl driven from the Nest that day with blows and curses. Somewhere in the leaves I would find her—and we would return to the city, her head garlanded with the red leaves of a chosen-one, and the same women who had stoned her forth would crowd about and welcome her when she returned. The fleeing woman looked over her shoulder with Kyla's eyes; and then the woman's form muted and Dr. Forth was standing between us in the tree-road, with the caduceus emblem on his coat stretched like a red staff between us. Kendricks in his Spaceforce uniform was threatening us with a blaster, and Regis Hastur was suddenly wearing a Space Service uniform too and saying, "Jay Allison, Jay Allison," as the tree-road splintered and cracked beneath our feet and we were tumbling down the waterfall and down and down and down . . .

"Wake up!" Kyla whispered, and dug an elbow into my side. I opened my eyes on crowded blackness, grasping at the vanishing nightmare. "What's the matter?"

"You were moaning. Touch of altitude sickness?"

I grunted, realized my arm was around her shoulder, and pulled it quickly away. After a while I slept again, fitfully.

Before light we crawled wearily out of the bivouac, cramped and stiff and not rested, but ready to get out of this and go on. The snow was hard, in the dim light, and the trail was not difficult here. After all the trouble on the lower slopes, I think even the amateurs had lost their desire for adventurous climbing; we were all just as well pleased that the actual crossing of Dammerung should be an anticlimax and uneventful.

The sun was just rising when we reached the pass, and we stood for a moment, gathered close together, in the narrow defile between the great summits to either side.

Hjalmar gave the peaks a wistful look.

"Wish we could climb them."

Regis grinned at him companionably. "Someday —and you have the word of a Hastur, you'll be along on that expedition." The big fellow's eyes glowed. Regis turned to me, and said warmly, "What about it, Jason? A bargain? Shall we all climb it together, next year?"

I started to grin back and then some bleak black devil surged up in me, raging. When this was over, I'd suddenly realized, I wouldn't be there. I wouldn't be anywhere. I was a surrogate, a substitute, a splinter of Jay Allison, and when it was over, Forth and his tactics would put me back into what they considered my rightful place—which was nowhere. I'd never climb a mountain except now, when we were racing against time and necessity. I set my mouth in an unaccustomed narrow line and said, "We'll talk about that when we get back—if we ever do. Now I suggest we get going. Some of us would like to get down to lower altitudes."

The trail down from Dammerung inside the ridge, unlike the outside trail, was clear and well-marked, and we wound down the slope, walking in easy single file. As the mist thinned and we left the snowline behind, we saw what looked like a great green carpet, interspersed with shining colors which were mere flickers below us. I pointed them out.

"The treetops of the North Forest—and the colors you see—are in the streets of the Trailcity."

An hour's walking brought us to the edge of the forest. We traveled swiftly now, forgetting our weariness, eager to reach the city before nightfall. It was quiet in the forest, almost ominously still. Over our heads somewhere, in the thick branches which in places shut out the sunlight completely, I knew that the tree-roads ran crisscross, and now and again I heard some rustle, a fragment of sound, a voice, a snatch of song.

"It's so dark down here," Rafe muttered, "anyone living in this forest would *have* to live in the treetops, or go totally blind!"

Kendricks whispered to me, "Are we being followed? Are they going to jump us?"

"I don't think so. What you hear are just the inhabitants of the city—going about their daily business up there."

"Queer business it must be," Regis said curiously, and as we walked along the mossy, needly forest floor, I told him something of the Trailmen's lives. I had lost my fear. If anyone came at us now, I could speak their language. I could identify myself, tell my business, name my foster parents. Some of my confidence evidently spread to the others.

But as we came into more and more familiar territory, I stopped abruptly and struck my hand against my forehead.

"I knew we had forgotten something!" I said roughly. "I've been away from here too long, that's all. Kyla."

"What about Kyla?"

The girl explained it herself, in her expressionless monotone. "I am an unattached female. Such women are not permitted in the Nests."

"That's easy then," Lerrys said. "She must belong to one of us." He didn't add a syllable. No one could have expected it; Darkovan aristocrats don't bring their women on trips like this, and their women are not like Kyla.

The three brothers broke into a spate of volunteering, and Rafe made an obscene suggestion. Kyla scowled obstinately, her mouth tight with what could have been embarrassment or rage. "If you believe I need your protection—!"

"Kyla," I said tersely, "is under *my* protection. She will be introduced as my woman—and treated as such."

Rafe twisted his mouth in an unfunny smile. "I see the leader keeps all the best for himself?"

My face must have done something I didn't know about, for Rafe backed slowly away. I forced myself to speak slowly. "Kyla is a guide, and indispensable. If anything happens to me, she is the only one who can lead you back. Therefore her safety is my personal affair. Understand?"

As we went along the trail, the vague green light disappeared. "We're right below the Trailcity," I whispered, and pointed upward. All around us the Hundred Trees rose, branchless pillars so immense that four men, hands joined, could not have circled one with their arms. They stretched upward for some three hundred feet, before stretching out their interweaving branches; above that, nothing was visible but blackness.

Yet the grove was not dark, but lighted with the

startlingly brilliant phosphorescence of the fungi growing on the trunks, and trimmed into bizarre ornamental shapes. In cages of transparent fibre, glowing insects as large as a hand hummed softly.

As I watched, a Trailman, quite naked except for an ornate hat and a narrow binding around the loins, descended the trunk. He went from cage to cage, feeding the glowworms with bits of shining fungus from a basket on his arm.

I called to him in his own language, and he dropped the basket, with an exclamation, his spidery thin body braced to flee or to raise an alarm.

"But I belong to the Nest," I called to him, and gave him the names of my foster parents. He came toward me, gripping my forearm with warm long fingers in a gesture of greeting.

"Jason? Yes, I hear them speak of you," he said in his gentle twittering voice, "you are at home. But those others—?" He gestured nervously at the strange faces.

"My friends," I assured him, "and we come to beg the Old One for an audience. For tonight I seek shelter with my parents, if they will receive us."

He raised his head and called softly, and a slim child bounded down the trunk and took the basket. The Trailman said, "I am Carrho. Perhaps it would be better if I guided you to your foster parents, so you will not be challenged."

I breathed more freely. I did not personally recognize Carrho, but he looked pleasantly familiar. Guided by him, we climbed one by one up the dark stairway inside the trunk, and emerged into the bright square, shaded by the topmost leaves, into a delicate green twilight. I felt weary and successful.

Kendricks stepped gingerly on the swaying, jiggling floor of the square. It gave slightly at every step, and Kendricks swore morosely in a language that fortunately only Rafe and I understood. Curious Trailmen flocked to the street and twittered welcome and surprise.

Rafe and Kendricks betrayed considerable contempt when I greeted my foster parents affectionately. They were already old, and I was saddened to see it; their fur greying, their prehensile toes and fingers crooked with a rheumatic complaint of some sort, their reddish eyes bleared and rheumy. They welcomed me, and made arrangements for the others in my party to be housed in an abandoned house nearby. They had insisted that I must return to their roof, and Kyla, of course, had to stay with me.

"Couldn't we camp on the ground instead?" Kendricks asked, eying the flimsy shelter with distaste.

"It would offend our hosts," I said firmly. I saw nothing wrong with it. Roofed with woven bark, carpeted with moss which was planted on the floor, the place was abandoned, somewhat musty, but weathertight and seemed comfortable to me.

The first thing to be done was to dispatch a messenger to the Old One, begging the favor of an audience with him. That done, (by one of my foster brothers), we settled down to a meal of buds, honey, insects and birds' eggs; it tasted good to me, with the familiarity of food eaten in childhood, but among the others, only Kyla ate with appetite and Regis Hastur with interested curiosity.

After the demands of hospitality had been satisfied, my foster parents asked the names of my party, and I introduced them one by one. When I named Regis Hastur, it reduced them to brief silence, and then to an outcry; gently but firmly, they insisted that their home was unworthy to shelter the son of a Hastur, and that he must be fittingly entertained at the Royal Nest of the Old One.

There was no gracious way for Regis to protest, and when the messenger returned, he prepared to accompany him. But before leaving, he drew me aside:

"I don't much like leaving the rest of you—"

"You'll be safe enough."

"It's not that I'm worried about, Dr. Allison."

"Call me Jason," I corrected angrily. Regis said, with a little tightening of his mouth, "That's it. You'll have to be Dr. Allison tomorrow when you tell the Old One about your mission. But you have to be the Jason he knows, too."

"So—?"

"I wish I needn't leave here. I wish you were— going to stay with the men who know you only as Jason, instead of being alone—or only with Kyla."

There was something odd in his face, and I wondered at it. Could he—a Hastur—be jealous of Kyla? Jealous of *me*? It had never occurred to me that he might be somehow attracted to Kyla. I tried to pass it off lightly.

"Kyla might divert me."

Regis said without emphasis. "Yet she brought Dr. Allison back once before." Then, surprisingly, he laughed. "Or maybe you're right. Maybe Kyla will —scare away Dr. Allison if he shows up."

CHAPTER VI

THE COALS of the dying fire laid strange tints of color on Kyla's face and shoulders and the wispy waves of her dark hair. Now that we were alone, I felt constrained.

"Can't you sleep, Jason?"

I shook my head. "Better sleep while you can." I felt that this night of all nights I dared not close my eyes or when I woke I would have vanished into the Jay Allison I hated. For a moment I saw the room with his eyes; to him it would not seem cozy and clean, but—habituated to white sterile tile, Terran rooms and corridors—dirty and unsanitary as any beast's den.

Kyla said broodingly, "You're a strange man, Jason. What sort of man are you—in Terra's world?"

I laughed, but there was no mirth in it. Suddenly I had to tell her the whole truth:

"Kyla, the man you know as me doesn't exist. I was created for this one specific task. Once it's finished, so am I."

She started, her eyes widening. "I've heard tales of—of the Terrans and their sciences—that they make men who aren't real, men of metal—not bone and flesh—"

Before the dawning of that naïve horror I quickly held out my bandaged hand, took her fingers in mine and ran them over it. "Is this metal? No, no, Kyla. But the man you know as Jason—I won't be he, I'll be someone different—" How could I explain

74

a subsidiary personality to Kyla, when I didn't understand it myself?

She kept my fingers in hers softly and said, "I saw someone else—looking from your eyes at me once. A ghost."

I shook my head savagely. "To the Terrans, I'm the ghost!"

"Poor ghost," she whispered.

Her pity stung. I didn't want it.

"What I don't remember I can't regret. Probably I won't even remember you." But I lied. I knew that although I forgot everything else, unregretting because unremembered, I could not bear to lose this girl, that my ghost would walk restless forever if I forgot her. I looked across the fire at Kyla, cross-legged in the faint light—only a few coals in the brazier. She had removed her sexless outer clothing, and wore some clinging garment, as simple as a child's smock and curiously appealing. There was still a little ridge of bandage visible beneath it and a random memory, not mine, remarked in the back corners of my brain that with the cut improperly sutured there would be a visible scar. *Visible to whom?*

She reached out an appealing hand. "Jason! Jason—?"

My self-possession deserted me. I felt as if I stood, small and reeling, under a great empty echoing chamber which was Jay Allison's mind, and that the roof was about to fall in on me. Kyla's image flickered in and out of focus, first infinitely gentle and appealing, then—as if seen at the wrong end of a telescope—far away and sharply incised and as remote and undesirable as any bug underneath a lens.

Her hands closed on my shoulders. I put out a groping hand to push her away.

"Jason," she implored, "don't—go away from me like that! Talk to me, tell me!"

But her words reached me through emptiness—I knew important things might hang on tomorrow's meeting, Jason alone could come through that meeting, where the Terrans for some reason put him through this hell and damnation and torture—oh yes —the Trailmen's fever—

Jay Allison pushed the girl's hand away and scowled savagely, trying to collect his thoughts and concentrate them on what he must say and do, to convince the Trailmen of their duty toward the rest of the planet. As if they—not even humans—could have a sense of duty!

With an unaccustomed surge of emotion, he wished he were with the others. Kendricks, now. Jay knew, precisely, why Forth had sent the big, reliable spaceman at his back. And that handsome, arrogant Darkovan—where was he? Jay looked at the girl in puzzlement; he didn't want to reveal that he wasn't quite sure of what he was saying or doing, or that he had little memory of what Jason had been up to.

He started to ask, "Where did the Hastur kid go?" before a vagrant logical thought told him that such an important guest would have been lodged with the Old One. Then a wave of despair hit him; Jay realized he did not even speak the Trailmen's language, that it had slipped from his thoughts completely.

"You—" he fished desperately for the girl's name,

"Kyla. You don't speak the Trailmen's language, do you?"

"A few words. No more. Why?" She had withdrawn into a corner of the tiny room—still not far from him—and he wondered remotely what his damned alter ego had been up to. With Jason, there was no telling. Jay raised his eyes with a melancholy smile.

"Sit down, child. You needn't be frightened."

"I'm—I'm trying to understand—" the girl touched him again, evidently trying to conquer her terror. "It isn't easy—when you turn into someone else under my eyes—" Jay saw that she was shaking in real fright.

He said wearily, "I'm not going to—to turn into a bat and fly away. I'm just a poor devil of a doctor who's gotten himself into one unholy mess." There was no reason, he was thinking, to take out his own misery and despair by shouting at this poor kid. God knew what she'd been through with his irresponsible other self—Forth had admitted that that damned "Jason" personality was a blend of all the undesirable traits he'd fought to smother all his life. By an effort of will he kept himself from pulling away from her hand on his shoulder.

"Jason, don't—slip away like that! *Think!* Try to keep hold on *yourself!*"

Jay propped his head in his hands, trying to make sense of that. Certainly in the dim light she could not be too conscious of subtle changes of expression. She evidently thought she was talking to Jason. She didn't seem to be overly intelligent.

"Think about tomorrow, Jason. What are you going to say to him? Think about your parents—"

Jay Allison wondered what they would think when they found a stranger here. He felt like a stranger. Yet he must have come, tonight, into this house and spoken—he rummaged desperately in his mind for some fragments of the Trailmen's language. He had spoken it as a child. He must recall enough to speak to the woman who had been a kind foster mother to her alien son. He tried to form his lips to the unfamiliar shapes of words—

Jay covered his face with his hands again. Jason was the part of himself that remembered the Trailmen. *That* was what he had to remember—Jason was not a hostile stranger, not an alien intruder in his body. Jason was a lost part of himself and at the moment a damn necessary part. If there were only some way to get back the Jason memories, skills, without losing *himself* . . . He said to the girl, "Let me think. Let me—" To his surprise and horror his voice broke into an alien tongue, "Let me alone, will you?"

Maybe, Jay thought, I could stay myself if I could remember the rest. Dr. Forth said Jason would remember the Trailmen with kindness, not dislike.

Jay searched his memory and found nothing but familiar frustration: years spent in an alien land, apart from a human heritage, stranded and abandoned. *My father left me. He crashed the plane and I never saw him again and I hate him for leaving me* . . .

But his father had not abandoned him. He had crashed the plane trying to save them both. It was no one's fault—

Except my father's. For trying to fly over the Hellers into a country where no man belongs . . .

He hadn't belonged. And yet the Trailmen, whom

78

he considered little better than roaming beasts, had taken the alien child into their city, their homes, their hearts. They had loved him. And he . . .

"And I loved them," I found myself saying half aloud, then realized that Kyla was gripping my arm, looking up imploringly into my face. I shook my head rather groggily. "What's the matter?"

"You frightened me," she said in a shaky little voice, and I suddenly knew what had happened. I tensed with savage rage against Jay Allison. He couldn't even give me the splinter of life I'd won for myself, but had to come sneaking out of my mind. How he must hate me! Not half as much as I hated him, damn him! Along with everything else, he'd scared Kyla half to death!

She was kneeling very close to me, and I realized that there was one way to fight that cold austere fish of a Jay Allison, send him shrieking down into hell again. He was a man who hated everything except the cold world he'd made his life. Kyla's face was lifted, soft and intent and pleading, and suddenly I reached out and pulled her to me and kissed her, hard.

"Could a ghost do this?" I demanded, "or this?"

She whispered, "No—oh, no," and her arms went up to lock around my neck. As I pulled her down on the sweet-smelling moss that carpeted the chamber, I felt the dark ghost of my other self thin out, vanish and disappear.

Regis had been right. It had been the only way.

The Old One was not old at all; the title was purely ceremonial. This one was young—not much older than I—but he had poise and dignity and the same strange indefinable quality I had recognized in Regis Hastur. It was something, I supposed, that the Terran Empire had lost in spreading from star to star—feeling of knowing one's own place, a dignity that didn't demand recognition because it had never lacked it.

Like all Trailmen he had the chinless face and lobeless ears, the heavy-haired body which looked slightly less than human. He spoke very low—the Trailmen have very acute hearing—and I had to strain my ears to listen, and remember to keep my own voice down.

He stretched his hand to me, and I lowered my head over it and murmured, "I make submission, Old One."

"Never mind that," he said in his gentle twittering voice. "Sit down, my son. You are welcome here, but I feel you have abused our trust in you. We dismissed you to your own kind because we felt you would be happier so. Did we show you anything but kindness, that after so many years you return with armed men?"

The reproof in his red eyes was hardly an auspicious beginning. I said helplessly, "Old One, the men with me are not armed. A band of those-who-may-not-enter-cities attacked us, and we defended ourselves. I traveled with so many men only because I feared to travel the passes alone."

"But does that explain why you have returned at all?" The reason and reproach in his voice made sense.

Finally I said, "Old One, we come as supplicants. My people appeal to your people in the hope that you will be—" I started to say, *as human*, stopped

80

and amended "—that you will deal as kindly with them as with me."

His face betrayed nothing. "What do you ask?"

I explained. I told it badly, stumbling, not knowing the technical terms, knowing they had no equivalents anyway in the Trailmen's language. He listened, asking a penetrating question now and again. When I mentioned the Terran Legate's offer to recognize the Trailmen as a separate and independent government, he frowned and rebuked me:

"We of the Sky People have no dealings with the Terrans, and care nothing for their recognition—or its lack."

For that I had no answer, and the Old One continued, kindly but indifferently, "We do not like to think that the fever which is a children's little sickness with us shall kill so many of your kind. But you cannot in all honesty blame us. You cannot say that we spread the disease; we never go beyond the mountains. Are we to blame that the winds change or the moons come together in the sky? When the time has come for men to die, they die." He stretched his hand in dismissal. "I will give your men safe-conduct to the river, Jason. Do not return."

Regis Hastur rose suddenly and faced him. "Will you hear me, Father?" He used the ceremonial title without hesitation, and the Old One said in distress, "The son of Hastur need never speak as a suppliant to the Sky People!"

"Nevertheless, hear me as a suppliant, Father," Regis said quietly. "It is not the strangers and aliens of Terra who are pleading. We have learned one thing from the strangers of Terra, which you have not yet learned. I am young and it is not fitting that

I should teach you, but you have said: 'Are we to blame that the moons come together in the sky?' No. But we have learned from the Terrans not to blame the moons in the sky for our own ignorance of the ways of the Gods—by which I mean the ways of sickness or poverty or misery."

"These are strange words for a Hastur," said the Old One, displeased.

"These are strange times for a Hastur," said Regis loudly. The Old One winced, and Regis moderated his tone, but continued vehemently, "You blame the moons in the sky. *I* say the moons are not to blame, nor the winds, nor the Gods. The Gods send these things to man to test their wits and to find if they have the will to master them!"

The Old One's forehead ridged vertically and he said with stinging contempt, "Is this the breed of king which men call Hastur now?"

"Man or God or Hastur, I am not too proud to plead for my people," retorted Regis, flushing with anger. "Never in all the history of Darkover has a Hastur stood before one of you and begged—"

"—for the men from another world."

"—for all men on our world! Old One, I could sit and keep state in the House of Hasturs, and even death could not touch me until I grew weary of living! But I preferred to learn new lives from new men. The Terrans have something to teach even the Hasturs, and they can learn a remedy against the Trailmen's fever." He looked round at me, turning the discussion over to me again, and I said:

"I am no alien from another world, Old One. I have been a son in your house. Perhaps I was sent to teach you to fight destiny. I cannot believe you are indifferent to death."

Suddenly, hardly knowing what I was going to do until I found myself on my knees, I knelt and looked up into the quiet, stern, remote face of the nonhuman.

"My father," I said, "you took a dying man and a dying child from a burning plane. Even those of their own kind might have stripped their corpses and left them to die. You saved the child, fostered him and treated him as a son. When he reached an age to be unhappy with you, you let a dozen of your people risk their lives to take him to his own. You cannot ask me to believe that you are indifferent to the death of a million of my people, when the fate of one could stir your pity!"

There was a moment's silence. Finally the Old One said, "Indifferent—no. But helpless. My people die when they leave the mountains. The air is too rich for them. The food is wrong. The light blinds and tortures them. Can I send them to suffer and die, those people who call me father?"

And a memory, buried all my life, suddenly surfaced. I said urgently, "Father, listen. In the world I live in now, I am called a wise man. You need not believe me, but listen; I know your people, they are my people. I remember when I left you, more than a dozen of my foster parents' friends offered, knowing they risked death, to go with me. I was a child; I did not realize the sacrifice they made. But I watched them suffer, as we went lower in the mountains, and I resolved—I resolved . . ." I spoke with difficulty, forcing the words through a reluctant barricade, ". . . that since others had suffered so for me . . . I would spend my life in curing the sufferings of others. Father, the Terrans call me a wise doctor, a man of healing. Among the Terrans I can see that my people, if they will come to us and help us, have air they can breathe and food which will suit them and that they are guarded from the light. I don't ask you to send anyone, father. I ask only —tell your sons what I have told you. If I know your people—who are my people forever—hundreds of them will offer to return with me. And you may witness what your foster son has sworn here; if one of your sons dies, your alien son will answer for it with his own life.

The words had poured from me in a flood. They were not all mine; some unconscious thing had recalled in me that Jay Allison had power to make these promises. For the first time I began to see what force, what guilt, what dedication working in Jay Allison had turned him aside from me. I remained at the Old One's feet, kneeling, overcome, ashamed of the thing I had become. Jay Allison was worth ten of me. Irresponsible, Forth had said. Lacking purpose, lacking balance. What right had I to despise my sober self?

At last I felt the Old One touch my head lightly.

"Get up, my son," he said, "I will answer for my people. And forgive me for my doubts and my delays."

Neither Regis nor I spoke for a minute after we left the audience room; then, almost as one, we turned to each other. Regis spoke first, soberly.

"It was a fine thing you did, Jason. I didn't believe he'd agree to it."

"It was your speech that did it," I denied. The sober mood, the unaccustomed surge of emotion, was still on me,—but it was giving way to a sudden upswing of exaltation. Damn it, I'd *done* it! Let Jay Allison try to match *that*.

Regis still looked grave. "He'd have refused, but you appealed to him as one of themselves. And yet it wasn't quite that—it was something more—" Regis put a quick embarrassed arm around my shoulders and suddenly blurted out, "I think the Terran Medical played hell with your life, Jason! And even if it saves a million lives—it's hard to forgive them for that!"

CHAPTER VII

LATE THE NEXT DAY the Old One called us in again, and told us that a hundred men had volunteered to return with us and act as blood donors and experimental subjects for research into the Trailmen's disease.

The trip over the mountains, so painfully accomplished, was easier in return. Our escort of a hundred Trailmen guaranteed us against attack, and they could choose the easiest paths.

Only as we undertook the long climb downward through the foothills did the Trailmen, unused to ground travel at any time, and suffering from the unaccustomed low altitude, begin to weaken. As we grew stronger, more and more of them faltered, and we traveled more and more slowly. Not even Kendricks could be callous about "inhuman animals" by the time we reached the point where we had left the pack horses. And it was Rafe Scott who came to me and said desperately, "Jason, these poor fellows will never make it to Carthon. Lerrys and I know this country. Let us go ahead, as fast as we can travel alone, and arrange at Carthon for transit—maybe we can get pressurized aircraft to fly them from here. We can send a message from Carthon, too, about accommodations for them at the Terran HQ."

I was surprised and a little guilty that I had not thought of this myself. I covered it with a mocking, "I thought you didn't give a damn about 'my friends'."

Rafe said doggedly, "I guess I was wrong about that. They're going through this out of a sense of duty, so they must be pretty different from the way I thought they were."

Regis, who had overheard Rafe's plan, now broke in quietly, "There's no need for you to travel ahead, Rafe. I can send a quicker message."

I had forgotten that Regis was a trained telepath. He added, "There are some space and distance limitations to such messages, but there is a regular relay net all over Darkover, and one of the relays is a girl who lives at the very edge of the Terran Zone. *If* you'll tell me what will give her access to the Terran HQ—" he flushed slightly and explained, "From what I know of the Terrans, she would not be very fortunate relaying the message if she merely walked to the gate and said she had a relayed telepathic message for someone, would she?"

I had to smile at the picture that conjured up in my mind. "I'm afraid not," I admitted. "Tell her to go to Dr. Forth, and give the message from Dr. Jason Allison."

Regis looked at me curiously—it was the first time

I had spoken my own name in the hearing of the others. But he nodded, without comment. For the next hour or two he seemed somewhat more preoccupied than usual, but after a time he came to me and told me that the message had gone through. Some time later he relayed an answer; that airlift would be waiting for us, not at Carthon, but at a small village near the ford of the Kadarin where we had left our trucks.

When we camped that night there were a dozen practical problems needing attention: the time and exact place of crossing the ford, the reassurance to be given to terrified Trailmen who could face leaving their forests but not crossing the final barricade of the river, the small help in our power to be given the sick ones. But after everything had been done that I could do, and after the whole camp had quieted down, I sat before the low-burning fire and stared into it, deep in painful lassitude. Tomorrow we would cross the river and a few hours later we would be back in the Terran HQ. And then . . .

And then—and then nothing. I would vanish, I would utterly cease to exist anywhere, except as a vagrant ghost troubling Jay Allison's unquiet dreams. As he moved through the cold round of his days, I would be no more than a spent wind, a burst bubble, a thinned cloud.

The rose and saffron of the dying fire gave shape to my dreams. Once more, as in the Trailcity that night, Kyla slipped through firelight to my side, and I looked up at her and suddenly I knew I could not bear it. I pulled her to me and muttered, "Oh Kyla —Kyla, I won't even remember you!"

She pushed my hands away, kneeling upright, and said urgently, "Jason, listen. We are close to

Carthon, the others can lead them the rest of the way. Why go back to them at all? Slip away now and never go back! We can—" she stopped, coloring fiercely, that sudden and terrifying shyness overcoming her again, and at last she said in a whisper, "Darkover is a wide world, Jason. Big enough for us to hide in. I don't believe they would search very far."

They wouldn't. I could leave word with Kendricks—not with Regis, the telepath would see through me immediately—that I had ridden ahead to Carthon, with Kyla. By the time they realized that I had fled, they would be too concerned with getting the Trailmen safely to the Terran Zone to spend much time looking for a runaway. As Kyla said, the world was wide. And it was my world. And I would not be alone in it.

"Kyla, Kyla," I said helplessly, and crushed her against me, kissing her. She closed her eyes and I took a long, long look at her face. Not beautiful, no. But womanly and brave and all the other beautiful things. It was a farewell look, and I knew it, if she didn't.

After the briefest time, she pulled a little away, and her flat voice was gentler and more breathless than usual. "We'd better leave before the others waken." She saw that I did not move. "Jason—"

I could not look at her. Muffled behind my hands, I said, "No, Kyla. I—I promised the Old One to look after my people in the Terran World."

"You won't be *there* to look after them! You won't be *you!*"

I said bleakly, "I'll write a letter to remind myself. Jay Allison has a very strong sense of duty. He'll look after them for me. He won't like it, but he'll do it, with his last breath. He's a better man than I am, Kyla. You'd better forget about me," I said, wearily. "I never existed."

That wasn't the end. Not nearly. She—begged, and I don't know why I put myself through the hell of stubborn refusal. But in the end she ran away, crying, and I threw myself down by the fire, cursing Forth, cursing my own folly, but most of all cursing Jay Allison, hating my other self with a blistering, sickening rage.

But before dawn I stirred in the light of the dying fire and Kyla's arms were around my neck in the darkness, her body pressed to mine, racked with convulsive crying.

"I can't convince you," she wept, "and I can't change you—and I wouldn't if I could. But while I can—while I can—I'll have you while you're you."

I crushed her to me. And for the moment my fear of tomorrow, my hate and bitterness against the men who had played with my life, were swept away in the sweetness of her mouth, warm and yielding, under mine. There in the light of the fading fire, desperate, knowing I would forget, I took her to me.

Whatever I might be tomorrow, tonight I was hers.

And I knew then how men feel when they love in the shadow of death—worse than death because I would live, a cold ghost of myself, through cold days and colder nights. It was fierce and savage and desperate; we were both trying to crowd a lifetime we could never have into a few stolen hours. But as I looked down at Kyla's wet face in the fading dawn, my bitterness had gone.

I might be swept away forever, a ghost, a nothing, blown away in the winds of one man's memory.

But to that last fading spark of memory, I would be forever grateful, and in my limbo I would be grateful, if ghosts know gratitude, to those who had called me from my nowhere to know this: these days of struggle and the love of comrades, the clean wind of the mountains in my face again, a last adventure, the warm lips of a woman in my arms.

I had lived more, in my scant week of life, than Jay Allison would live in all his white and sterile years. I had had my lifetime. I didn't grudge him his, any more.

Coming through the outskirts of the small village, next afternoon, the village where the airlift would meet us, we noted that the poorer quarter was almost deserted. Not a woman walked in the street, not a man lounged along the curbing, not a child played in the dusty squares.

Regis said bleakly, "It's begun," and dropped out of line to stand in the doorway of a silent dwelling. After a minute he beckoned to me, and I looked inside.

I wished I hadn't. The sight would haunt me while I lived. An old man, two young women and half a dozen children between four and fifteen years old lay inside. The old man, one of the children, and one of the young women were laid out neatly in clean death, shrouded, their faces covered with green branches after the Darkovan custom for the dead. The other young woman lay huddled near the fireplace, her coarse dress splattered with the filthy stuff she had vomited, dying. The children—even now I can't think of the children without retching. One, very small, had been in the woman's arms when she collapsed; it had squirmed free—for a little while. The others were in an indescribable condition, and the worst of it was that one of them was still moving, feebly, long past help. Regis turned blindly from the door and leaned against the wall, his shoulders heaving—not, as I first thought, in disgust, but in grief. Tears ran over his hands and spilled down, and when I took him by the arm to lead him away, he reeled and fell against me.

He said in a broken, blurred, choking voice, "Oh, Gods, Jason, those children, those children—if you ever had any doubts about what you're doing, any doubts about what you've done, think about that, think that you've saved a whole world from that, think that you've done something even the Hasturs couldn't do!"

My own throat tightened with something more than embarrassment. "Better wait till we know for sure whether the Terrans can carry through with it, and you'd better get to hell away from this doorway. I'm immune, but damn it, you're not." But I had to take him and lead him away, like a child, from that house. He looked up into my face and said with burning sincerity, "I wonder if you believe I'd give my life, a dozen times over, to have done that?"

It was a curious, austere reward. But vaguely it comforted me. And then, as we rode into the village itself, I lost myself, or tried to lose myself, in reassuring the frightened Trailmen who had never seen a city on the ground, never seen or heard of an airplane. I avoided Kyla. I didn't want a final word, a farewell. We had had our farewells already.

Forth had done a marvelous job of preparing quarters for the Trailmen, and after they were comfortably installed and reassured, I went down wearily and dressed in Jay Allison's clothing. I looked out the window at the distant mountains and a line from the book on mountaineering, which I had bought as a youngster in an alien world, and Jay had kept as a stray fragment of personality, ran in violent conflict through my mind:

Something hidden—go and find it . . .
Something lost beyond the ranges . . .

I had just begun to live. Surely I deserved better than this, to vanish when I had just discovered life. Did the man who did not know how to live, deserve to live at all? Jay Allison—that cold man who had never looked beyond any ranges—why should I be lost in him?

Something lost beyond the ranges—nothing would be lost but myself. I was beginning to loathe the overflown sense of duty which had brought me back here. Now, when it was too late, I was bitterly regretting—Kyla had offered me life. Surely I would never see Kyla again.

Could I regret what I would never remember? I walked into Forth's office as if I were going to my doom. I *was*—

Forth greeted me warmly.

"Sit down and tell me all about it," he insisted. I would rather not have spoken. Instead, compulsively, I made it a full report—and curious flickers came in and out of my consciousness as I spoke. By the time I realized I was reacting to a post-hypnotic suggestion, that in fact I was going under hypnosis again, it was too late and I could only think that this was worse than death because in a way I would be alive.

Jay Allison sat up and meticulously straightened his cuff before tightening his mouth in what was meant for a smile. "I assume, then, that the experiment was a success?"

"A complete success." Forth's voice was somewhat harsh and annoyed, but Jay was untroubled; he had known for years that most of his subordinates and superiors disliked him, and had long ago stopped worrying about it.

"The Trailmen agreed?"

"They agreed," Forth said, surprised. "You don't remember anything at all?"

"Scraps. Like a nightmare." Jay Allison looked down at the back of his hand, flexing the fingers cautiously against pain, touching the partially healed red slash. Forth followed the direction of his eyes and said, not unsympathetically, "Don't worry about your hand. I looked at it pretty carefully. You'll have total use of it."

Jay said rigidly, "It seems to have been a pretty severe risk to take. Did you ever stop to think what it would have meant to me, to lose the use of it."

"It seemed a justifiable risk, even if you had," Forth said dryly. "Jay, I've got the whole story on tape, just as you told it to me. You might not like having a blank spot in your memory. Want to hear what your alter ego did?"

Jay hesitated. Then he unfolded his long legs and stood up. "No, I don't think I care to know." He waited, arrested by a twinge of a sore muscle, and frowned.

What had happened, what would he never know, why did the random ache bring a pain deeper than the pain of a torn nerve? Forth was watching him, and Jay asked irritably, "What is it?"

"You're one hell of a cold fish, Jay."

"I don't understand you, sir."

"You wouldn't," Forth muttered. "Funny. I *liked* your subsidiary personality."

Jay's mouth contracted in a mirthless grin.

"You would," he said, and swung quickly around.

"Come on. If I'm going to work on that serum project I'd better inspect the volunteers and line up the blood donors and look over old whatshisname's papers."

But beyond the window the snowy ridges of the mountain, inscrutable, caught and held his eye; a riddle and a puzzle—

"Ridiculous," he said, and went to his work.

CHAPTER VIII

FOUR MONTHS LATER, Jay Allison and Randall Forth stood together, watching the last of the disappearing planes, carrying the volunteers back toward Carthon and their mountains.

"I should have flown back to Carthon with them," Jay said moodily. Forth watched the tall man stare at the mountain; wondered what lay behind the contained gestures and the brooding.

He said, "You've done enough, Jay. You've worked like the devil. Thurmond, the Legate, sent down to say you'd get an official commendation and a promotion for your part. That's not even mentioning what you did in the Trailmen's city." He put a

94

hand on his colleague's shoulder, but Jay shook it off impatiently.

All through the work of isolating and testing the blood fraction, Jay had worked tirelessly and unsparingly; scarcely sleeping, but brooding; silent, prone to fly into sudden savage rages, but painstaking. He had overseen the Trailmen with an almost fatherly solicitude—but from a distance. He had left no stone unturned for their comfort—but refused to see them in person except when it was unavoidable.

Forth thought, we played a dangerous game. Jay Allison had made his own adjustment to life, and we disturbed that balance. Have we wrecked the man? He's expendable, but damn it, what a loss! He asked, "Well, why *didn't* you fly back to Carthon with them? Kendricks went along, you know. He expected you to go until the last minute."

Jay did not answer. He had avoided Kendricks, the only witness to his duality. In all his nightmare brooding, the avoidance of anyone who had known him as Jason became a mania. Once, meeting Rafe Scott on the lower floor of the HQ, he had turned frantically and plunged like a madman through halls and corridors, to avoid coming face to face with the man, finally running up four flights of stairs and taking shelter in his rooms, with the pounding heart and bursting veins of a hunted criminal. At last he said, "If you've called me down here to give me hell about not wanting to make another trip into the Hellers—!"

"No, no," Forth said equably, "there's a visitor coming. Regis Hastur sent word he wants to see you. In case you don't remember him, he was on Project Jason—"

"I remember," Jay said grimly. It was nearly his one clear memory—the nightmare of the ledge, his slashed hand, the naked body of the Darkovan woman, —and blurring these things, the too-handsome Darkovan aristocrat who had banished him for Jason again. "He's a better psychiatrist than you are, Forth. He changed me into Jason in the flicker of an eyelash, and it took you half a dozen hypnotic sessions."

"I've heard about the psi powers of the Hasturs," Forth said, "but I've never been lucky enough to meet one in person. Tell me about it. What did he do?"

Jay made a tight movement of exasperation, too controlled for a shrug. "Ask him, why don't you. Look, Forth, I don't much care to see him. I didn't do it for Darkover; I did it because it was my job. I'd prefer to forget the whole thing. Why don't you talk to him?"

"I rather had the idea that he wanted to see you personally. Jay, you did a tremendous thing, man! Damn it, why don't you strut a little. Be—be normal for once! Why, I'd be damned near bursting with pride if one of the Hasturs insisted on congratulating me personally!"

Jay's lip twitched, and his voice shook with controlled exasperation. "Maybe you would. I don't see it that way."

"Well, I'm afraid you'll have to. On Darkover nobody refuses when the Hasturs make a request—and certainly not a request as reasonable as this one." Forth sat down beside the desk. Jay struck the woodwork with a violent clenched fist and when he

96

lowered his hand there was a tiny smear of blood along his knuckles. After a minute he walked to the couch and sat down, very straight and stiff, saying nothing. Neither of the men spoke again until Forth started at the sound of a buzzer, drew the mouthpiece toward him, and said, "Tell him we are honored—you know the routine for dignitaries, and send him up here."

Jay twisted his fingers together and ran his thumb, in a new gesture, over the ridge of scar tissue along the knuckles. Forth was aware of an entirely new quality in the silence, and started to speak to break it, but before he could do so, the office door slid open on its silent beam, and Regis Hastur stood there.

Forth rose courteously and Jay got to his feet like a mechanical doll jerked on strings. The young Darkovan ruler smiled engagingly at him.

"Don't bother, this visit is informal; that's the reason I came here rather than inviting you both to the Tower. Dr. Forth? It is a pleasure to meet you again, sir. I hope that our gratitude to you will soon take a more tangible form. There has not been a single death from the Trailmen's fever since you made the serum available."

Jay, motionless, saw bitterly that the old man had succumbed to the youngster's deliberate charm. The chubby, wrinkled old face seamed up in a pleased smile as Forth said, "The gifts sent to the Trailmen in your name, Lord Hastur, were greatly welcomed."

"Do you think that any of us will ever forget what they have done?" Regis replied. He turned toward the window and smiled rather tentatively at the man who stood there motionless since his first conventional gesture of politeness.

"Dr. Allison, do you remember me at all?"

"I remember you," Jay Allison said sullenly.

His voice hung heavily in the room, its sound a miasma in his ears. All his sleepless, nightmare-charged brooding, all his bottled hate for Darkover and the memories he had tried to bury, erupted into overwrought bitterness against this too-ingratiating youngster who was a demigod on this world and who had humiliated him, repudiated him for the hated Jason. For Jay, Regis had suddenly become the symbol of a world that hated him, forced him into a false mould.

A black and rushing wind seemed to blur the room. He said hoarsely, "I remember you all right," and took one savage, hurtling step.

The weight of the unexpected blow spun Regis around, and the next moment Jay Allison, who had never touched another human being except with the remote hands of healing, closed steely, murderous hands around Regis' throat. The world thinned out into a crimson rage. There was shouting, and sudden noises, and a red-hot explosion in his brain . . .

"You'd better drink this," Forth remarked, and I realized I was turning a paper cup in my hands. Forth sat down, a little weakly, as I raised it to my lips and sipped. Regis took his hand away from his throat and said huskily, "I could use some of that, doctor."

I put the whisky down. "You'll do better with

water until your throat muscles are healed," I said swiftly, and went to fill a throwaway cup for him, without thinking. Handing it to him, I stopped in sudden dismay and my hand shook, spilling a few drops. I said hoarsely, swallowing, "—but drink it, anyway."

Regis got a few drops down, painfully, and said, "My own fault. The moment I saw—Jay Allison—I knew he was a madman. I'd have stopped him sooner only he took me by surprise."

"But—you say *him*—I'm Jay Allison," I said, and then my knees went weak and I sat down. "What in hell is this? I'm not Jay—but I'm not Jason, either—"

I could remember my entire life, but the focus had shifted. I still felt the old love, the old nostalgia for the Trailmen; but I also knew, with a sure sense of identity, that I was Doctor Jason Allison, Jr., who had abandoned mountain climbing and become a specialist in Darkovan parasitology. Not Jay who had rejected the world; not Jason who had been rejected by it. But then who?

Regis said quietly, "I've seen you before—once. When you knelt to the Old One of the Trailmen." With a whimsical smile he said, "As an ignorant superstitious Darkovan, I'd say that you were a man who'd balanced his god and daemon for once."

I looked helplessly at the young Hastur. A few seconds ago my hands had been at his throat. Jay or Jason, maddened by self-hate and jealousy, could disclaim responsibility for the other's acts.

I couldn't.

Regis said, "We could take the easy way out, and arrange it so we'd never have to see each other again. Or we could do it the hard way." He extended his hand, and after a minute, I understood, and we shook hands briefly, like strangers who have just met. He added, "Your work with the Trailmen is finished, but we Hasturs committed ourselves to teach some of the Terrans our science—matrix mechanics. Dr. Allison—Jason—you know Darkover, and I think we could work with you. Further, you know something about slipping mental gears. I meant to ask: would you care to be one of them? You'd be ideal."

I looked out the window at the distant mountains. This work—this would be something which would satisfy both halves of myself. The irresistible force, the immovable object—and no ghosts wandering in my brain. "I'll do it," I told Regis. And then, deliberately, I turned my back on him and went up to the quarters, now deserted, which we had readied for the Trailmen. With my new doubled—or complete—memories, another ghost had roused up in my brain, and I remembered a woman who had appeared vaguely in Jay Allison's orbit, unnoticed, working with the Trailmen, tolerated because she could speak their language. I opened the door, searched briefly through the rooms, and shouted, "Kyla!" and she came. Running. Disheveled. Mine.

At the last moment, she drew back a little from my arms and whispered, "You're Jason—but you're something more. Different—"

"I don't know who I am," I said quietly, "but I'm me. Maybe for the first time. Want to help me find out just who that is?"

I put my arm around her, trying to find a path

between memory and tomorrow. All my life, I had walked a strange road toward an unknown horizon. Now, reaching my horizon, I found it marked only the rim of an unknown country.

Kyla and I would explore it together.

The Waterfall

by
Marion Zimmer Bradley

The lady Sybil-Mhari, fifteen years old and as frail as a branch of willow, stood at the edge of an enclosed courtyard, staring with pensive gray eyes into the valley, flooded with the strange moonlight of the four moons. A low wall of stone, barely knee-high, was the only thing dividing the court where she stood from a steep, sheer and hazardous cliff that dropped away sharply to a raging, foaming torrent of white water that fell, nearly a thousand feet, into the valley. The muffled roar of water beneath her, and the cold moon-flooded night, cut through her with the dampness that rose from the waterfall far below, seemed to tremble hotly in her young body, twisting a thick lump in her throat, a feeling that was like hunger or thirst—or something else. . . . Something she could not even guess; a hunger, a loneliness, for something she had never known.

Love? No. Her waiting-women chattered and squealed of love continually, whispering together, giggling confidences of stolen kisses and furtive

touches, of seeking hands in the darkness, of courtly
verses and songs. And for a little while Sybil had
believed it was, indeed, love for which she hun-
gered; but as confidences had grown more definite,
they had evoked neither excitement nor longing, but
only a shudder of disgust. What—she, Sybil-Mhari
Aillard, *comynara,* the delicate and queenly little
sister of the Lord Ludovic, lonely and perfect as a
single star, to surrender herself to these hungry indecencies? She, born into the caste of Comyn, apart
and above, bearing—so the common folk said—the
blood of Gods, *she* to swoon in the arms of some
clumsy esquire, to lend herself to secret kissings,
fumbling fingers, whispered words of love, in corridor or hall or chapel? No. And no. The hunger
that was in her was surely for something other than
this; it was as a burning fire seeking fuel, and these
huggings and clutchings were damp and common-
place, smothering instead of feeding the flame.

She looked down at the white water that coursed
and plunged and raced, throwing up silvery spray
so far beneath her that the water seemed all one
whiteness in the moonlight, and suddenly imaged
herself flying, falling through that vast space, into
the race and torrent; whirled, battered, drowned—
or would she, as some old legends said that the
Comyn folk could do, put forth sudden wings, fly
wingless far above the world, wheeling on hawk-
pinions, looking down from far above. . . . But that
was legend. Or dream. She hugged herself with thin
bare arms and clutched dizzily at the wall, almost
hypnotized by the tumult and sound of the distant
waterfall. To fly, borne on invisible wings, or the
secret powers of the Comyn, aloft, above everyone

who sought to pin her down and keep her earthbound . . . but that was long ago. Legend.

Now the Comyn held only the powers of the mind, and even those she had been denied. The *leronis*, the great sorceress of Hastur blood, had called Sybil to her but this year, had made her look into the starstone, so that Sybil felt she stood more naked than if the woman had stripped from her the last garment, feeling the touch of the *leronis* on her mind. Sybil had stood unflinching, not daring to show fear; but inside her something cowered and wept and could not raise its eyes, and at last the *leronis* had sighed and put away the stone. "You have *laran*, my child; you bear the Gift of our clan. And yet . . ." the woman sighed again, and shook her head. "There is a power in you, Sybil, that I do not understand; and yet I had thought I knew all the Gifts of Comyn. You are telepath—not greatly, but enough. You could be trained in a Tower; could wield all the power of a *leronis*, perhaps a Keeper. Yet something in me—something I have come to trust—says . . . *no*."

Sybil had protested "Why, lady?" There was a sullen anger in her. The women of the Towers wielded power and force, they used the trained powers of the mind—all other women of the Comyn were powerless, given in marriage and forced to bear children for their clan, but wielding no power of their own . . . and the *leronis* would deny her this! Rage had surged in her, but she made her voice sweet and docile as she had been taught, and murmured, in the voice that her brother Ludovic, lord of the clan, had said was like the gentle murmuring of a green rainbird, "Why, lady? I am *comynara*, I have *laran*, you yourself have said it . . . why?"

But the Hastur sorceress only shook her head, meeting Sybil's eyes with a flash that told the girl that the older woman knew, and did not fear, all of her hidden rage. She said, "Because your mind is not the mind of a woman, Sybil; it holds something other than *laran*. I do not know what it is, but I fear it; and I fear you; and I will not have you in a Tower. If you are to master the craft of the star-stones, if you are to wield all the ancient powers of the Comyn, I must know, absolutely, that you are to be trusted. So I say no."

And then Sybil had raised her eyes and glared at the woman and had thrust forth a power she did not know was in her, to seize the woman, to compel her will upon her—*I will have this power*. The woman had pushed her mind away easily, and had shaken her head with a sad laugh. "You see, my poor child? I do not fear you as you are now; but I fear what you might be, wielding the craft of the starstones." And she had gone away, taking with her Sybil's young foster-sister Rohana, to be brought to the Tower and trained in the craft of the starstones, and Sybil had been left here to loneliness, and hunger, and melancholy, and the aching need of something . . . something, she could not guess what it might be. . . .

After a long time, aware that she was cramped and chilled to the bone, she straightened and slowly turned away. Behind her lay the Comyn castle, a great and sprawling mass of stone and echoing silence; the empty courtyards gave resonant sighs as her silk-shod feet whispered on the flag-stones, and even her own breathing seemed to stir an echoing murmur. The icy cold of the stones crept up her stiffened legs and throbbed in her breasts.

From very far away Sybil heard a halt, a clash, a challenge, the echo of ringing steps and silence; the Guardsmen were making their nightly rounds. Hurrying her steps a little, she slipped shadowlike under an archway, sheltering against the chilly night breeze; then she started, catching her hands to her throat with a little squeak of surprise as a light, thrust abruptly forward, rayed harshly across her face.

Half blinded, she pressed her fingers over her eyes; then as her pupils slowly adjusted to the light, she lowered her hands to see a man's face above the crude flare of the lantern.

"Well, now! Look what I found!"

Sybil shrank back as the unfamiliar face spread into a wide grin. The voice was deep and harsh, almost hoarse, but it sounded good-natured. "What are you doing here, you?"

The spreading light was less painful to Sybil's eyes now. She could distinguish black leather straps on a green cloak; one of the Guardsmen who came from their homes, at Council season, to guard the Comyn lords and ladies. She had seen them from time to time; they bowed deeply as she passed, and lowered their eyes in humility when, as sometimes happened, she spoke some condescending word or gave some minor command. But this was one she had never seen before—and never before had one of them dared to address her uninvited, by so much as a word.

She said coldly, "Go about your business, fellow."

"Easy there, wench," the man chuckled, "My business is right here, see; finding out who goes in and out of this court. What's yours?"

Sybil's small white teeth clamped in her lip. It

would be too humiliating to identify herself to this
. . . this roughneck! She saw that he was a thickset
man, with a heavy neck and burly broad shoulders,
and his grin, through the untidily sprouting whis-
kers, showed very long, strong white teeth like a
horse's!

"I live here," she said shortly.

The man laughed. "And so do a dozen other
women, but I'll take your word for it. Come, give
us a kiss, *chiya,* and I'll let you go." He bent and
deliberately set the lantern on the ground, then deliberately stepped toward her, and Sybil—too frozen
in astonishment to move—felt his rough hands on
her bare arms. The hoarse, chuckling voice was very
close to her ear.

"Who were you looking for, girl, won't I do instead?"

Paralyzed, a horrid sick emptiness clawing inside
her belly, Sybil felt the rough arms around her waist,
felt her feet leave the ground as he caught her up
bodily against his chest, and the stubbled face
scraped hard against her soft cheek. For a moment
she hung limp, unable to move a muscle—this
couldn't be happening! Then, in a convulsion of terror, she exploded like a frantic cat, arching backward, silently clawing at her captor. She opened
her mouth to scream, but her dry throat would give
voice only to a little whimper of terror.

"Take it easy, hell-cat!" the strange voice muttered in the half-dark. She felt rough and weathered fingers searching the silks and ribbons that con-
fined her breast, and her voice came back in a choking scream.

"Put me down! How dare you? You'll be flayed
alive for this!"

Something in her imperious command, even through the shrillness of hysteria, came through to the man, and he set her abruptly on her feet, snatching up the lantern. "Zandu's hells," he swore, *"Who are you?"*

She swayed as he released her, dizziness blurring her eyes, and caught for support at the rough stonework, steadying herself with a hand flattened against the wall. Her voice sounded high and strange in her own ears.

"I am Sybil-Mhari Aillard," she said hoarsely, "and the Lord Ludovic will have the skin stripped from your body in ribbons an inch wide!"

"Domna!" The man's voice was husky and disbelieving. He said protestingly, "But . . ." and he sagged and leaned back. A curious little stab, like a cramp in her belly, sharp but somehow not unpleasant, suddenly weakened Sybil's knees again as she contemplated his whitening face. He stared, gulped audibly once or twice. After a moment he managed to collect himself somewhat, the hoarse voice was puzzled and apologetic, but if Sybil had expected him to cringe—and she had—she was oddly disappointed.

"My lady, I must beg your forgiveness. I took you for a serving-girl—and what in the name of the Blessed Cassilda," he finished rationally, "are you doing, my lady, out here in the courtyard in the night air, in your smock like any wench from the kitchens?"

Sybil blinked, put oddly on the defensive. She started to say, I wanted to look at the waterfall, but then she realized she need not explain herself to a common Guardsman! The doings of a Comyn lady were no concern of his! He was holding the lantern close to her face, and his own features emerged more clearly—rough-cut and bronzed, an old scar seaming his cheek, but with twinkling eyes that even now looked good-humored. His breath was none too steady as he said "Well, my little lady, it's perfectly sure I'd be buzzard meat if you wanted to make trouble for me, but you wouldn't do a thing like that, would you? I meant no harm, you know, and after all, who'd expect the Lady Sybil-Mhari to be roaming about the courtyard after moonrise?" His smile was coaxing, almost intimate. "I can only say I'm sorry—or maybe I'm not," he finished suddenly. "If you'd not told me who you were, maybe I'd have wanted more than a kiss, and taken it too!"

Sybil swayed slightly, feeling—as she had felt when she looked into the starstone—the strange alien touch against her mind . . . *Desire* . . . *Fear*. . . . His hot eyes were still fastened on her, searching through the untied ribbons at her bosom, but hesitant, somehow held back . . . *fear*. She could feel his fear . . . and the desire, burning into her, burning *through* her . . . he dared not touch her now
. . . .

She swayed slightly, and, this time without apology, he put his arms behind her shoulders, bent to support her light weight.

She whispered "I feel . . . faint. . . ." and let herself fall limp against him, her head dropping pliantly into the hollow of his shoulder; she could feel the slow pounding of his heart through his jerkin, she could feel . . . she buried her forehead still more closely into the heat of him. *There is a power in you*, the *leronis* had said. Now, feeling its surge, she knew what lay behind his fear and desire; her

110

hands felt icy cold, and, shivering, she caught one of his warm ones and pressed it to her throat.

"I . . . I can't breathe," she whispered, making her voice soft, beguiling. She made sure, before releasing his hand, that he would not be able to let her go again. She closed her eyes, as he lifted her; hung suspended, it seemed, swaying between air and fire, and felt again the strange ecstatic sensation of hurling, tumbling, flying, falling—the waterfall roaring beneath.

When she opened her eyes, he had laid her down in a sheltered grass-plot opening from one of the courtyards and was kneeling beside her, his rough hands working, with deft blunt motions, on the ribbons imprisoning her breast. She breathed deeply and whispered "Now I feel better—I don't know what happened to me. . . ." But when he would have drawn his hands hesitantly away again, she captured and held them.

"No, no . . . don't let me go," she begged, feeling the cold, emptiness surge back again. She was frightened, sick with the fear she felt in him, and yet compelled by something more powerful still, something building. . . . She did not know what it was, was it only this? Then his arms were around her again, disbelieving, hungry, gentle, and his mouth forcing her lips apart.

It was strange, shaking and strange, the surge and tremble that overwhelmed her. Never before had she known any touch like this; the fumbling and sweatily respectful hand-kiss of her cousins, the cold fatherly hand of the Lord of the Domain on her brow, the giggling embrace of her girl-companions—nothing like this rough hunger, so tender for all its fierceness. "My little lady," he whispered huskily, against her throat. "You don't even know what it is you want, do you?"

No. But I will know, I will. . . . The memory spun in her, *there is a power in you, and I fear it . . .* but could it be only this, only this? She fastened her mouth to his, biting savagely at his stiff lips, struggling furiously—not in protest, but in eagerness, against the gentle pressure of his hands. There was a writhing, a straining, a moment of agony; she felt the dew damp on her back, icy cold through the thin silk of her dress, his heavy rough hairiness drowning her silken breasts. She twisted and fought, not with any desire to escape, but rather in the same savage determination with which she fought to grip an untamed horse with her thin thighs, the same grim conflict with which she struggled to hood an unruly falcon. She knew what was happening to him, she knew what was happening to her, but it was not what she thought, it was only a beginning, as she felt all his fear, respect, hesitation, sink down and die beneath the growing urgency, need, hunger. . . .

She pushed away his hot kisses as the man's spent breathing hissed past his parted teeth, and sat up, retying her shoulder-ribbons with flying fingers. Was this the final ineffable joy, the delight immeasurable, about which the other maidens squealed and whispered? She pushed his hand away when he would have assisted her, her whole body flinching in revulsion. She felt bruised and shaken, and she clenched her teeth tight to keep them from chattering. She broke into his whispered stream of endearments with a quick, shaken, "Take me back—they will be looking for me."

He raised her gently, as he might pick up a child who has stumbled, and she drew a deep breath, something . . . she hardly knew what . . . growing to swift birth inside her tight, throbbing breasts, her bruised and aching body. She forced herself to conceal her shaking, and to smile up at him, then leaned her head hard against his encircling arm and murmured with deliberate pathos, "You must take me back—I am almost a prisoner, you know."

He supported her faltering steps, half carrying her, whispering, "Yes, yes, my little silken bird, my little flower." He paused at the edge of the archway, retrieving his lantern from its hiding-place, and looked at her, saying hesitantly, "Little lady, you cannot return like this!"

In the crude light Sybil looked down at her crushed and torn ribbons, her crumpled and stained dress, tasting the blood on her lips with a slow satisfaction. She touched her tangled coppery curls with exploring fingers as he persuaded, "Come, little one, smooth your dress, let me fasten your sash. No one must see you like this!" There was fear in him again, and she could feel it like a taste in her mouth. Sybil tilted her head to one side, then heard the sound for which, without knowing it until this moment, she had been waiting. The clash of pikes, the ringing step and the challenge. She clenched her small fists, feeling her breath roughen and catch in her throat, smiling up at him.

"Must they not?" she murmured, then suddenly whirled, breaking away from him, and cried out imperiously, "Guard! Guard, to me!"

"What . . ." the man took a backward step; booted feet, running, echoed in harsh sequence on the flagstones and an explosion of lights burst in

their faces; the face of a steel-capped Guard—
*Blessed Cassilda be thanked! It's a Guard who
knows me by sight!*—thrust through the archway
and a startled voice gasped "Lady Sybil-Mhari!"

She pointed, with a dramatic gesture, feeling the
frightening power surge up inside her. "Kill him!"
she commanded, and heard her voice breaking on
what she herself would have taken for a wild sob
of shame and fright, if she had heard it from another throat. She could almost see herself reflected
in the Guard's eyes, in his mind, swollen lips oozing
a trace of bitten blood, the loosened ribbons falling
to show her bruised breast, the skirt torn to show a
hint of narrow thighs. The Guard spat out a cry of
dismay and horror, shouting to his confederates;
Sybil turned away, modestly mantling her face with
her hair, as a second Guard appeared behind the
first and his face echoed all the changes she had
seen in the first. A tiny smile of contempt trembled
on Sybil's lips, but she made it into a piteous
grimace, widening her eyes as she looked down at
the man in whose arms she had lain only a few
minutes ago. She whispered pathetically "The Lord
Ludovic must never know—my honor is in your
hands—but how can it be? But if he were . . . somehow . . . to fall into the waterfall. . . ."

And now she saw the blanching of terror, the
whitening of nostril and jaw, as the man's eyes
sought hers in wild entreaty.

"Lady . . . little lady. . . ." he gasped helplessly,
and his hoarse and husky voice, as when he had
whispered endearments, sent a thrill of warmth
through her.

*There is a power in you . . . and I fear it . . .
oh,* she thought ecstatically, *if the Hastur sorceress*

*could only know . . . she would have robbed me
of this. . . .*

She watched the Guards seize the man, expertly
pinion his arms; followed like a shadow, hugging
herself with her thin arms, on the crest of rising excitement, as they hustled him rudely toward the
cliff. He was shouting now, hoarse indecencies, until one of the Guards shoved a hand over his mouth.
They struggled briefly at the wall, and suddenly
Sybil felt a wild thrill surging through her body. It
knifed hotly through her breasts, overwhelming as
a kiss; stabbed fluid warmth all through her, gripped
her thighs in a vise of pleasure. She gasped, her
breath jolting out on the cresting heat of it, and
cried aloud in unbearable delight as the man's figure tottered on the ledge, clawed wildly at the air,
flailed and disappeared. Sybil sank down in the
grass, breathing in heavy sobs, knowing now what
was the true power, the joy of love—vaguely, in her
overwhelming surge of emotion, she wondered what
his name had been, how she could discover his
name. She would remember it always in her prayers
for the dead, the name of the one who had released
the power within her, had brought her to fulfillment.
She became aware that one of the Guards was bend-
ing solicitously over her. She was too spent to rise;
she let him lift her, leaning heavily on his arm, swaying helplessly.

"Lady Sybil," he said gently, "Your honor, and
your secret, are forever safe with me. I will conduct
you safe to the women's quarters; see you only that
your maids do not gossip, and this night's work shall
never be known." He guided her tottering steps with
reverent hands. "Poor little lady, if I had been at
hand, that beast, that disgrace to the Guards and

their honor, had never dared lay his hands on you
. . ."

She lowered her long lashes. "What is your name?
I would thank my . . . my preserver in my prayers,
before I sleep."

"Reuel, my lady."

"Reuel. I shall . . . remember," she whispered.
She would not make that mistake again. "You will
not find me . . . ungrateful." Again the unendur-
able pleasure gusted up through her as she saw his
thin swarthy face go foolish and soft with a sudden,
incredible hope. She murmured, "I often walk in
the courtyard here. Will you protect me?"

"With . . . with my very life, Lady." he stam-
mered, and she looked at him and smiled. With him
the terror need not strike till she had fed on the desire for a day or two, and the fear, and the hope
. . . till she had fed herself full. Now that she knew
her power, she could wait for her pleasure.

She smiled, with the drunken joy of a woman who
has discovered true love, and ran lightly up the stairway toward her chamber.

CLIFFORD D. SIMAK

10624	**City**	$1.75
77220	**So Bright the Vision**	$1.50
81002	**Time and Again**	$1.75
82442	**The Trouble With Tycho**	$1.50

Available wherever paperbacks are sold or use this coupon.

★ ★ ★ ★ ★

MARION ZIMMER BRADLEY